The Truth of It

Fall From Grace
Book 3

Beth Orsoff

ISBN: 979-8-9887329-2-1 (paperback)

www.bethorsoff.com

Also by Beth Orsoff:

Romantically Challenged

Disengaged

Honeymoon for One

Girl in the Wild

Vlad All Over

Vlad to the Bone

Game Changer

The Billionaire Who Wasn't

Boy Toy

Fall From Grace

The Lies We Tell

Prologue

Today is the two-year anniversary of my husband and daughter's death, and if all goes according to plan, I'll soon be meeting the man responsible for their murder. He didn't pull the trigger himself; that man is already dead. But for this man, my family would be alive today. The fact that they are dead and he is free to live his life is an unacceptable outcome. And I intend to do everything in my power to change it.

Chapter 1

It was an unusually warm day for February. So warm I left my coat in the car when I walked up the hill to my husband and daughter's graves. I placed the bright bouquet of Gerber daisies in front of Amelia's headstone. The pink, yellow, and orange flowers seemed more appropriate for a child. I placed the bouquet of white roses on Jonah's grave then sat down on the grass in front of their headstones.

First, I told them about Sofia. She and I had grown closer in the few months since she and MJ moved back into my aunt's house. I'd made an effort to connect with Sofia this time, and it paid off. She talked to me now almost as much as she talked to my aunt and MJ. I was trying to help Sofia learn to read, which she was struggling with. I'd already met with her kindergarten teacher to express my concern, but the teacher insisted Sofia was fine and some children just learned more slowly than others. I wasn't buying it. Getting Sofia tested for learning disabilities was next on my to do list.

Next I brought them up to speed on MJ, my aunt, and my mother. Then I turned to Jonah's grave and told him what I intended to do this morning when I left the cemetery. I asked

Jonah for his blessing, which he gave me, although it's not as if I gave him a choice in the matter.

After I told them both I loved them, I walked back to my car. Visiting Jonah and Amelia was always hard, but over time, it had gotten a little easier. As I started the engine, I glanced into my rearview mirror and caught sight of their identical side-by-side headstones. If I had any doubts about what I planned to do today, that convinced me I was making the right decision.

I exited the cemetery and drove directly to the courthouse. My client was in the infirmary and would not be joining me in the courtroom today, a fact I was not unhappy about. The less time I had to spend with him the better. I had not felt this way about my previous clients, but my previous clients had not been arrested for selling fentanyl-laced marijuana to teenagers.

Although I'd been a practicing attorney for eight years, this was my first foray into criminal defense work. I'd spent the past couple of months preparing by reviewing my notes and outlines from my criminal law and procedure classes in law school and watching trials at the courthouse. I wanted to be ready when the perfect case presented itself. This was the case, the one we had all been waiting for. And by "we," I meant me, Alex, and FBI Special Agent Roberto Diaz.

Did my client commit the crime he was accused of? Yes. Was I trying to get him off anyway? Yes. Was it immoral? Before my family was gunned down on a suburban street in broad daylight, what I referred to as my Before life, I would've acknowledged while every criminal defendant is entitled to the presumption of innocence and a competent defense, I would never have agreed to provide that defense. It would've been unthinkable to me. But now I lived in After, and in After I'd learned to embrace moral complexity, if not by choice, then by necessity. Helping a low-level drug dealer evade conviction was a price I was willing to pay to get justice for my family. It would be the first of many acts unimaginable Before, but in After, it was just another day at the office.

When the clerk called my case, I walked through the swinging doors separating the well of the courtroom from the public benches and took my place at the defense table. I was fully prepared to argue that my Motion to Suppress Evidence should be granted because it violated my client's Fourth Amendment rights. But the judge had evidently read my brief beforehand because she immediately turned to the Assistant District Attorney and asked why she *shouldn't* grant my motion. He tried, but the facts were not on his side and the judge ruled in my favor. With the evidence from the illegal search excluded, the ADA had nothing left. Neither of us was surprised when the judge granted my Motion to Dismiss too.

I walked out of the courtroom first and ADA Nathan Hale followed. I tried not to smile as we shook hands. No one likes an arrogant winner.

"Are you new to the area?" he asked as other lawyers brushed past us in the crowded hallway. "I don't think I've ever seen you before."

He may not have seen me, but I'd seen him. I'd sat in on one of his trials last week. Because I was just another spectator in the gallery, he hadn't noticed me. He'd done a good job, I'd thought, which meant the defendant was found guilty.

"No," I said, "just new to criminal defense work."

ADA Nathan Hale smiled. He came off as friendly and sincere and not at all smarmy, good attributes for a trial attorney. "That explains it. Beginner's luck."

I laughed. "Or just good lawyering."

He glanced at his watch. "I should go. You never want to be late in Judge Deary's courtroom. He's an ornery bastard."

"Good to know," I said.

Then ADA Hale pulled a small leather billfold out of his

jacket pocket and handed me a business card. "If you ever want to get on the right side of justice, call me. We can always use more good lawyers on our side of the aisle."

"Will do," I said and slipped his card into my briefcase. *If he only knew...*

Chapter 2

ADA HALE WOULD NEVER KNOW he and I were already working on the same side of the aisle. The only people who knew the truth were Alex, my aunt, and a handful of agents at the FBI.

I pulled my phone out of my purse and texted Alex: *Case dismissed.*

He knew what to do next.

It was three days later when Alex called me. "Yo, counselor."

I could hear other people murmuring in the background, so I knew he had me on speakerphone. "Yo, Alex."

"You done right by my homey."

"Thanks," I said, saving the document I'd been working on and closing the file. "You can return the favor by paying my bill, which you'll be receiving shortly."

"Don't I always pay?"

"Usually."

Alex, Agent Diaz, and I had devised this plan months ago. Now that I'd gotten the charges against Alex's associate dropped, the next move was his.

"I was bragging on you to a friend of mine," Alex continued. "He wants to meet."

"What kind of friend?" I asked.

"The kind who pays his lawyer's bills too."

"I'm listening."

"He's what you'd call an entrepreneur. Lives down here in LA."

"You know I don't travel farther than the county line."

"What have you got against LA?"

"Nothing except for the hours I'd have to waste sitting in traffic getting there and back."

"I'm sure my friend would make it worth your while."

"No thanks," I said, "but call me next time one of your pals gets arrested in Santa Veneta." Then I hung up before Alex could respond.

We'd scripted that conversation too. Alex was afraid if I seemed too eager, his friend, the Russian mob boss, would get suspicious. Agent Diaz agreed.

"You need to play hard to get," Alex had advised when the three of us met two weeks ago at a fast-food restaurant halfway between Santa Veneta and LA. It had become our unofficial meeting spot these past few months where we hashed out the details of our plan. Agent Diaz had picked it because it was far enough away from all our homes and offices that the odds of any of us running into someone we knew were infinitesimal. Plus, we all loved the french fries.

Alex leaned back against the hard plastic booth and smirked. "I know you know how to play hard to get."

I gave him a hard stare and reached for the fries. I was used to Alex's innuendo. I'd been ignoring it since the day we'd met, the morning after I'd brought his niece and nephew to live with me and my Aunt Maddy.

"Igor's going to have such a hard on for you," he continued.

"And why would you think that's a good thing?" I asked. "You think I want some old man chasing me around a desk?"

Alex dipped a french fry into his ketchup. "Don't worry. You're too old for him."

"*I'm* too old for *him*?" I was thirty-three, which meant I was twenty-five years younger than Igor Volodnik.

"Igor likes 'em young," Agent Diaz said and popped a ketchup-less french fry into his mouth.

"Ew." As if I didn't already hate this man enough, now I learn he's a pedophile too.

"Not underage," Agent Diaz said. "Igor's too careful for that. He likes them barely legal, then dresses them up to look like they aren't."

"All the thrills of statutory rape without the jail time?" I quipped.

Agent Diaz laughed. "Exactly."

"What a charming man," I replied.

"Actually, he is," Agent Diaz said. "Or he can be. Just make sure you stay on his good side."

I intended to—right up until the moment I stuck the knife in his back. Figuratively, of course. Although I'd fantasized about killing Igor Volodnik many times, I never would. Besides not having it in me to actually commit murder, I recalled my criminal procedure professor's advice. "It is your ethical obligation to zealously represent your client to the best of your abilities," he used to tell us. "But when the cell door slams shut, make sure you're on the outside." I thought it was good advice when I was in law school and I still thought so today.

Agent Diaz turned to Alex. "You think he'll introduce her to Mischa?"

"Mischa is Igor's son," Alex explained. "Igor brings in women for him all the time, but rumor is Mischa plays for the other team, like your friends Tim and Richard."

I gave Alex another hard stare. He'd broken our unspoken rule. Alex and I didn't talk about Tim and Richard, MJ and Sofia's former foster parents. I thought they were great and was still friendly with them. Alex had nothing against them personally, he was just a homophobe.

"Then I guess I don't need to worry about Mischa chasing me around the desk either," I said.

I turned to Agent Diaz, who was staring off into the middle distance. I'd spent enough time with him now that I knew that meant he was thinking. "What?" I asked.

Agent Diaz turned to me. "If Mischa is gay, it could work to our advantage."

"How?" I asked.

"Igor would never admit to having a gay son," Agent Diaz replied. "It's just not acceptable in Russian culture. That's why he keeps bringing in women for Mischa."

"What does that even mean?" I asked. "Bringing in women? From where? And why bother if Mischa's gay?"

"Mischa might not be interested in you sexually," Agent Diaz continued, "but you can still be useful to him. And him to you."

"Because he despises his father as much as I do and wants to send him to prison for the rest of his life too?" I asked.

Alex chuckled but Agent Diaz didn't even crack a smile. "Mischa would never betray his father. He knows if he did, he'd be a dead man."

I said, "Then what are you suggesting?"

"Become his beard," Agent Diaz replied. "His pretend girlfriend."

"I know what a beard is," I said. "And I can see how that might help him, but how does it help me? I'm trying to get Igor to hire me as his defense attorney, not date his son."

"There's no reason you can't do both," Agent Diaz said.

"And being Mischa's girlfriend, even his fake girlfriend, would make this operation safer for you."

"Because Igor's less likely to suspect me?" I doubted that, especially if Igor knew his son was secretly gay.

"You may find this hard to believe," Alex said, "but some of the guys in Igor's crew aren't as gentlemanly as me."

I rolled my eyes. "You don't think I know how to handle unwanted advances?" I'd been handling his for the last nine months.

Agent Diaz leaned in. "Grace, you need to take this seriously. For some of these guys, saying no is like waving a red flag in front of a bull."

"Are you trying to scare me out of doing this? Because it's not going to work. I'm committed. And I'm sure even the Neanderthals who work for Igor can tell the difference between a female attorney and a prostitute." I assumed it was prostitutes Igor was bringing in from god-knows-where to do god-knows-what to his gay son to try to turn him straight.

Alex chuckled again. "You think those guys are gonna be looking at your briefcase? They ain't. They're gonna be staring at your tits and your ass, just like every other woman they see."

I turned to Agent Diaz and waited for him to contradict Alex. Instead, he said, "He's right. Every guy on Igor's crew needs to know you're off limits. If you can't interest Mischa, then we'll move on to Plan B."

"What's Plan B?" I asked.

"You can be Alex's fake girlfriend instead."

Chapter 3

I'D WAITED until Sofia and MJ had gone to bed to relay my conversation with Alex and Agent Diaz to Aunt Maddy, who hooted with laughter. "Alex would love that!"

Agent Diaz would be furious if he found out I was discussing any of this with my aunt, which is why I had no intention of telling him. When the FBI first agreed to bring me on as a confidential informant, Agent Diaz had been very clear I could not tell anyone. "For their safety as well as yours," he'd said. But I'd already told my aunt about my plan before the FBI agreed, so in my mind, she was grandfathered in. But I still took Agent Diaz's admonition to heart. I didn't tell Aunt Maddy everything, and I was careful never to talk to her about it in front of the kids.

"I wouldn't be his real girlfriend," I said. "It would just be part of my cover to keep Igor's men from hassling me."

Aunt Maddy laughed harder.

"It's true!" I cried. "No one agrees to testify against the mob just to sleep with someone!"

"Okay, sweetheart," Aunt Maddy said, refilling her wine-glass and topping off mine. "Whatever you say. Just do us both a favor and don't come home pregnant. Because that would be a lot harder to explain away to your mother."

Several days passed before Alex called again. I knew it was him before I answered because he was calling on my second cell phone, the one he'd given me and only he knew the number.

"Where are you?" he asked.

"On my way home," I replied as I locked my office door behind me. "Why?"

"Your aunt's house or yours?"

"My aunt's." I'd moved back in with my aunt when she'd started fostering MJ and Sofia again.

"Go to your house instead. I don't want the kids to see me and start asking questions."

I unlocked my car door and slid in. "You're coming up here? Why? Has something happened?"

"Igor sent me to pick you up. You're having dinner with him tonight at his restaurant."

That statement prompted so many questions I wasn't sure where to start. "Isn't it customary to ask someone if they can make it first before sending someone to pick them up? What if I had plans for tonight?" I didn't, unless you counted having dinner with my aunt and the kids, giving Sofia a bath and reading to her, and helping MJ with his homework. But Igor didn't know that.

"This isn't a date. When Igor Volodnik invites you to dinner at his restaurant, you go."

"Igor owns a restaurant?" I knew about the drugs, the gambling ring, the credit card scams, the extortion, and the money laundering. Agent Diaz had neglected to mention Igor was a restaurateur too.

"Yeah," Alex said. "Real fancy place. Maybe you've been there."

"I don't think I've ever eaten at a Russian restaurant before."

"It's not Russian. It's one of those celebrity joints. The name's Lava."

The traffic light ahead of me turned yellow and instead of speeding up, I slammed on my brakes, forcing the driver behind me to swerve around me so he could run the light. He shot me the bird as he drove past, but I didn't reciprocate. I was too focused on my conversation with Alex to indulge in reciprocal road rage. "Igor Volodnik owns Lava!"

I'd never been to Lava, but I knew the name, as did anyone who'd ever read a celebrity gossip magazine. I assumed from the many photos I'd seen of celebrities entering and exiting the restaurant's infamous red leather doors that the paparazzi permanently camped out front.

"Co-owns," Alex said. "He's a silent partner. Very silent."

I wondered if all the famous people who frequented Lava knew they were dining at a restaurant partly owned by a Russian crime boss. If they did, would they stop eating there? Or would the criminal connection make the place more glamorous and they'd want to be seen there even more?

"What would happen if I told Igor I had other plans tonight?" I had no intention of turning down the invitation. I was just curious.

"You'd change your plans," Alex said.

"What if I didn't want to?"

Alex sighed. "Grace, if you've changed your mind about this—"

"I haven't. It's just..." Although I'd spent every waking hour of the last few months plotting the downfall of Igor Volodnik, now that I would finally be meeting the man who was responsible for my family's murder, I was terrified. Not just of what he might do to me if he found out I was an FBI informant, but of what I might do to him. I despised this man with every fiber of my being. I wasn't sure how I was going to react when I finally met him face to face. But I swallowed hard and said, "What should I wear?"

"How the hell should I know. I'm not one of your gay boys."

I rolled my eyes even though Alex couldn't see me.

"Just look pretty," he said.

"What does it matter? I thought I was too old for Igor."

"You are," Alex replied. "But that doesn't mean he won't enjoy the view."

Chapter 4

"Wow," Alex said when I opened my front door.

I looked down at my navy dress. It wasn't especially low cut or clingy, but it fit me well and could be dressed up or down depending on the occasion. In the past I'd paired it with a blazer and pumps and worn it to court. Tonight, I donned silver high-heeled sandals, dangly earrings, and the diamond bracelet Jonah had given me on our last wedding anniversary. It was the first time I'd worn the bracelet since Jonah died.

"You said to look pretty," I replied.

"You do," Alex said, still staring.

I supposed I should've been flattered, but I wasn't. I found Alex's attention unsettling. I grabbed my silver wrap and evening bag off the entryway table and said, "We should go. I'm sure Igor doesn't like to be kept waiting."

I HADN'T PLANNED on napping on the drive down to LA. I'd been practicing my mindful breathing to quell my anxiety and apparently relaxed myself so much I fell asleep. When I awakened, we were exiting the 405 freeway at Sunset Boulevard.

"You ready for this?" Alex asked as we sped east along the winding road, which on this end of town was flanked on both sides by gated driveways, tall hedges, and mansions set far back from the street.

"No." I felt like I might vomit.

"Relax. You got this."

I definitely did not have this, and there was no way I could relax. I turned away from him and stared out the passenger side window, watching as the red brick buildings of UCLA gave way to the mansions of Beverly Hills. Then we crossed into West Hollywood and the scenery abruptly changed. This was the Sunset Boulevard everyone knew from countless movies and TV shows—the famous clubs, the glowing neon signs, and the ever-present paparazzi.

Alex pulled his BMW to a stop in front of Lava. Before I could open my door, the valet opened it for me. I stepped out onto the sidewalk and a photographer immediately pointed his camera at me, then dropped it when he realized I wasn't a celebrity. I was grateful for his disinterest, but it didn't quell my anxiety. I was starting to feel lightheaded. That's when Alex appeared at my side. He grabbed my arm and held me upright. "Do me a favor," he whispered. "If you're gonna puke, warn me first."

"Do I look like I'm gonna puke?" I heard the words and knew they came out of my mouth, but my head felt detached from my body.

"Yes," he said, right before I leaned over into a flower bed and vomited. When I stopped heaving, Alex pulled me upright and propelled me through the restaurant's famous red leather doors. Then he dragged me down a long hallway and stopped in front of a black door with the universal symbol for the women's restroom in red glitter. "Go fix yourself up and decide if you really want to do this," he said. "It's not too late to back out."

"It is too late. We're already here."

"It's not," he insisted. "But you need to decide now." Then he pushed open the ladies room door and nudged me inside.

I stumbled into a stall, hiked up my dress, and sat down on the toilet with my head in my hands. *Why on earth did I think I could do this?*

Because you can.

I can't.

You can and you will.

I can't.

Then I caught sight of the diamond bracelet sparkling on my wrist, and I could practically hear Jonah's voice in my head. *Feel the fear and do it anyway.* I laughed out loud. Jonah loved reading those business-y self-help books. I used to tease him about it all the time. I bet he repeated those words to himself before he met with Volodnik too.

Yeah, and look how well that turned out.

But he still did it, didn't he? He felt the fear and he did it anyway because he loved his brother and would do anything for him.

And you loved Jonah and Amelia. Nothing you do will bring them back, but you can get justice for them. Don't you owe them that?

I heard the ladies room door bang open and then Alex's voice call my name. I jumped up from the toilet and flushed even though I hadn't peed and stepped out of the stall. It was just the two of us in the restroom, but I still said, "You can't be in here."

"Decision time," Alex said and held up his phone, which was buzzing with a number I didn't recognize. "It's Igor. Are you doing this or not?"

Chapter 5

I TRIED NOT to gape as we weaved our way through the tables in the restaurant's opulent dining room. I'd already recognized one aging movie star and a woman who hosted a daytime television talk show. Igor was sitting alone at a square table in the corner with his back to the wall. I couldn't see his face because he was staring down at his phone, but I recognized him by his strangely dyed hair. It was jet black on top with wide white-gray strips on either side of his head, like a skunk in reverse. He wore an expensive looking suit with a white shirt open at the collar where a tuft of black and gray chest hair peeked out. Then Igor looked up from his phone and our eyes met.

I felt like I was inside the dance scene from *West Side Story* where Tony and Maria first spot each other across the crowded room, except instead of my heart filling with desire, it filled with hate.

This man murdered my family. This man destroyed my life. This man has to pay.

As I followed the maître d', we passed a table set with a large, serrated steak knife. I actually considered grabbing it so I could use it to stab Igor through the heart. But I stifled the impulse.

As we approached Igor's table, he stood up. His lips were moving and he was definitely speaking, but it was Jonah's voice I heard in my head. *Eyes on the prize, Grace. Eyes on the prize.* I swallowed my revulsion, forced a smile on my lips, and shook Igor Volodnik's outstretched hand. I was so lightheaded I didn't know how I managed to remain upright.

I hate you. I hate you. I hate you. You should be dead, and Jonah and Amelia should be alive. You have no right to live. I could strangle you with my bare hands.

STOP THIS NOW. Focus. Think. Use your brain. If you want to beat him, then you need play the long game. Rein in your emotions and breathe. Just breathe.

Igor continued talking. I smiled and nodded but I didn't hear a word he said. It wasn't until the maître d' pulled out my seat that I noticed the table, which had four chairs, only contained two place settings. I'd just assumed Alex would be joining us for dinner. I was barely holding myself together, I was definitely not prepared to do this alone. Alex must've seen the panic on my face, because he quickly pulled out the chair next to mine and sat down.

I glanced at Igor. First his bushy eyebrows rose in surprise, then he let out a raucous laugh. In Russian-accented English he told the maître d', "We'll be four for dinner tonight. Get Sergey. He's at the bar."

"Right away, sir," the maître d' replied then disappeared.

Within seconds a busboy appeared and added two more place settings. Igor was speaking to Alex and I was so focused on my breathing I didn't even notice the tall man with the shaved head until he was standing at Igor's side. He was facing away from me so all I could see of him, besides his dark jacket and his smooth skull, was the black tattoo covering the back of his neck. It looked like a bird of some kind, although not one I recognized.

Then the tattooed man turned around and Igor introduced us. "Sergey, this is Grace."

His eyes were black, his skin chalky white, and his cheek bones jutted out sharply. He looked like the grim reaper minus the robe and scythe. The fear must've shown on my face because Igor let out another raucous laugh and patted my shoulder with his meaty hand. "Relax, sweetheart. He doesn't bite." Then he glanced at Sergey. "Don't stand there like a dolt. Say hello."

Sergey offered me his hand. As soon as my skin touched his, I shivered. His fingers were even colder than I imagined they would be. Although, to be fair, he had been holding a beer.

"Sit," Igor said to him. "You're eating with me tonight."

Sergey's eyebrows shot up, so I knew the invitation, or really the order, surprised him, but he stayed silent as he took his seat. He and Alex nodded at each other, so I assumed the two were already acquainted.

When the hovering waiter approached our table, Igor said, "Bring us a bottle of vodka and four glasses."

"Just water for me," I replied. I didn't want to drink anything tonight that could dull my senses.

"In Russia everyone drinks vodka," Igor said. "Is like water."

I smiled as sweetly as I could. "In America only water is water." Then I looked up at the waiter and said, "Sparkling if you have it. Any brand is fine."

"Are you an alcoholic?" Igor asked.

I considered lying and telling him I was, but I was afraid to. The point of this awful exercise was to get Igor to hire me. He might not if he thought I was an alcoholic, even a recovering one. Although now that I'd met Igor, I wasn't sure I was actually going to be able to go through with this anyway. How could I work for the man responsible for my family's murder?

Because you have no choice.

"No," I replied.

"Then you'll drink with me," Igor said.

I turned to Alex, whose expression was inscrutable, but under the table he placed his hand on my knee and squeezed. We hadn't discussed secret hand signals on the drive down from Santa Veneta, but I took the gesture to mean, *do what he wants.*

The waiter returned with a chilled bottle of vodka and four rocks-size glasses, no ice. Igor poured a generous amount of alcohol into each glass and held his up, so the three of us lifted our glasses too. Igor said something in Russian, which I assumed was a toast, then in English said, "To our friendship."

Igor downed his entire glass in one gulp. I took a small sip from mine and felt the alcohol burn its way down my throat and into my chest. But instead of dulling my senses, it focused me.

You will smile and nod and pretend to like this man. You will do this for Jonah and Amelia. You will do this because your love for them is stronger than your hate for the man responsible for their death.

When I turned back to Igor, he was already pouring himself another.

I NURSED my one glass of vodka through an heirloom tomato salad, oysters on the half-shell, and crispy Sichuan sea bass with spicy green beans and polenta. I assumed that the restaurant deserved its stellar reviews and the food really was excellent, but I barely tasted it. I was on edge the whole meal waiting for Igor to question me. I knew this dinner was a job interview of sorts. But while Igor frequently glanced in my direction, he rarely spoke to me. He spent almost the entire meal talking to

Sergey and Alex about work. He complained about supply issues and logistical problems and that their margins were being squeezed by upstart competitors. If I didn't know better, I would think this was a legitimate business dinner. Igor didn't ask me a single question that wasn't about the food until the waiter brought our coffee and dessert.

"So how come you're not married?" Igor asked, briefly glancing down at my cleavage before returning his gaze to my face.

Showtime. I set down my dessert fork next to my mostly uneaten flourless chocolate cake and forced myself to smile. "I guess I haven't met the right man yet."

Igor swatted away my answer as if it was a fly buzzing in front of his face. "You women. Always looking for Mr. Right."

"What's wrong with looking for Mr. Right?" I nodded to the wide gold band on his ring finger, which for some reason he wore on his right hand instead of his left. "Didn't you look for Mrs. Right before you married her?"

Igor set down his fork and pointed to his wedding ring. "This is third Mrs. Right." He let out a boisterous laugh. Sergey and Alex chuckled and I forced a polite smile. Then Igor picked up his fork again and stabbed the center of his pear tart. "You're thirty-three. You should be married."

I wasn't shocked Igor knew my age—Agent Diaz had told me Igor would look into my background before we met. That's why he made me delete all my social media accounts and switch back to using my maiden name. He also arranged for the FBI to scrub my public records. Agent Diaz didn't want Igor to find any information that could link me back to Jonah or Jake.

"You sound like my mother," I replied.

"She must be a wise woman." Igor grinned.

"I'll be sure and tell her you said so."

Igor laughed and took a huge bite of his pear tart. "Alex tells me you're a good lawyer."

I swallowed a small bite of chocolate cake before I replied. "I do okay."

"Don't be modest," Igor said. "I know you went to fancy law school and worked at big law firm—until you vanished."

The friendly Igor disappeared, replaced by the menacing version. But Agent Diaz had prepared me for this too. "I didn't vanish. I moved to Santa Veneta."

Igor leaned back in his chair and folded his arms across his barrel chest. "Why?"

That's when Alex chimed in. "I told you. Grace—"

Igor held up his hand and Alex stopped talking. "I want to hear it from her."

I picked up my sparkling water, which was now flat, and stared back at him. I silently thanked Agent Diaz, who had insisted we rehearse my cover story over and over again, so when Igor asked me these questions, I could answer them without thinking, like I would if I was telling the truth.

I took a sip of my water and set the glass down. "If you must know, I left because of a bad breakup. I needed a change of scenery, so I quit my job and backpacked around Europe until I ran out of money. When I came back, I needed a place to live, so I moved in with my aunt. It was either that or live with my mother and my aunt seemed like the lesser of two evils."

Igor nodded as if I was confirming a story he already knew. "When are you moving back to LA?"

"I'm not." I turned to Alex, whose expression was, as usual, inscrutable. "Didn't Alex tell you?"

"You're young," Igor scoffed. "You should live in big city where you have opportunity, not some sleepy little town."

I bristled at his characterization of my adopted home.

"Santa Veneta's a city too, just smaller than LA. And there are people there I don't want to leave."

Whether to disclose my relationship with MJ and Sophia was something that had been hotly debated between me, Alex, and Agent Diaz. I wanted to keep the kids out of this. All the legal filings were in my aunt's name, so Igor wouldn't know I was connected to them unless we told him, I'd argued. But Alex thought Igor would trust me more if he knew he and I shared a personal connection. Agent Diaz agreed and pointed out it would be easy enough for Igor to have me followed and discover the truth himself. Then, if Alex or I hadn't told Igor—and Agent Diaz decided it would be better if it came from me—it would look like I was hiding something and ultimately put us both in danger.

Igor's eyebrows shot up. "Boyfriend?"

I shook my head. "Children. My aunt and I are foster parents to Alex's niece and nephew. That's how we met."

Igor glanced at Alex then back at me. "Alex lives in LA."

"Well, obviously my maternal instinct is stronger than his."

Igor laughed. "Then you should all move to LA! The children can be closer to their uncle too."

"No. The kids are staying in Santa Veneta." I'd told Agent Diaz the same when he suggested I move back to LA for the duration of the investigation. It was one of the points I'd dug in on since he'd agreed to let me be a confidential informant. "They're doing well in school and I don't want to move them. And their biological mother lives in Santa Veneta. She has visitation rights, *court-ordered* visitation rights, so we can't move."

Igor slapped his hand on the table, and I jumped. "How are you going to work for me if you insist on living two hours away?"

I swallowed hard and said, "I didn't realize I was working for you."

"That's why you're here, no?" Igor said.

My heart started pounding in my chest. *Breathe. Just breathe.* "To be honest, I'm not sure why I'm here. Alex said you wanted to meet me, so I came. I'd be happy to have you as a client, but if you're not interested because I live in Santa Veneta, then I'll leave." I pushed my chair away from the table and stood up.

"Sit," Igor ordered.

I remained standing. I reminded myself of Alex's admonition. *If you want Igor to trust you, you have to play hard to get.* Igor had to believe I was willing to walk away.

"Please," Igor said and motioned for me to sit down again.

I didn't think he would ask a third time, so I returned to my seat. Igor stared at me, and I tried to keep my face neutral, neither challenging him, nor cowering in fear—at least on the outside. On the inside I was terrified.

"You're tough cookie," he finally said. "I like that. But I need you in LA."

"Why? I can just drive down for court appearances. Everything else I can do from my office in Santa Veneta." I'd made this pitch to Alex and Agent Diaz too and eventually they'd relented.

"What court appearances?" Igor asked.

"I'm a criminal defense attorney," I said. "Surely, Alex told you that."

"I already have good defense attorney," Igor said.

I turned to Alex, who didn't react, then back to Igor. "Then why did you want to meet me?"

"I have other job in mind for you."

Chapter 6

Alex pulled into the Ralphs grocery store parking lot and parked under the street lamp with the burned out bulb. Agent Diaz was already waiting for us two spots over in his nondescript dark sedan. When Alex shut off the engine, Agent Diaz exited his car and slipped into Alex's back seat.

"How'd it go?" Agent Diaz asked.

I turned to Alex, but he continued to stare straight ahead, so I did too.

After thirty seconds of silence Agent Diaz said, "One of you better answer me or I'm pulling the plug on this right now."

I turned around in my seat so I was facing him. "Igor wants to hire me, but not as his defense attorney."

"Then as what?" Agent Diaz asked.

"His son's babysitter," I spat, then spun around so I was staring out the windshield again.

"Not his babysitter," Alex said. "His business partner."

"There is no point in me doing any of this if my job is to hold Mischa's hand," I replied, continuing the argument we'd been having since we left the restaurant. "I'm here to get evidence on Igor. I gather the evidence and give it to you, you give it to the FBI, the government prosecutes Igor, you testify against him at trial, Igor goes to jail for the rest of his life. None of that is going to happen if I'm stuck babysitting Mischa. And I'm not going to be his beard either. If Igor knows he's gay, he'll never believe it anyway."

"I told you this was a bad idea," Alex said. "But you wouldn't listen, because you never listen."

"*I* never listen? You're one to talk."

"Enough!" Agent Diaz said. "You two sound like my in-laws, and they've been making each other miserable for forty years."

Alex gripped the steering wheel, his knuckles white, and stared out the windshield. I folded my arms across my chest and looked out the passenger-side window. For a while no one spoke. Then Agent Diaz said, "Okay, Plan A is off the table. We move on to Plan B."

"Which is?" I asked.

"You partner with Igor's son," Agent Diaz said.

"But—"

Agent Diaz held up his hand to stop me. "Listen to me, Grace. You do not need to be Igor's defense attorney to get us the evidence we need. There is no reason to think Mischa's business is any more legitimate than his father's. Even if it looks that way on the surface, odds are something shady is happening underneath. Your job will be to find out what that something is." Then Agent Diaz turned to Alex, who was still facing forward but watching our exchange in the rearview mirror. "Your job remains the same."

"What's his job?" I asked.

It was Alex who answered. "To keep you from getting yourself killed."

Neither of us spoke on the drive back to Santa Veneta. When Alex dropped me off at my house, he sped away before

I'd even made it to my front door. I thought about driving to my aunt's house but it was already late and I didn't want to wake the kids, so I texted her and told her I was sleeping at my place tonight and I'd be back in the morning.

Sleeping alone? she texted.

Yes, I texted back and silenced the phone.

Aunt Maddy was feeding the kids breakfast when I arrived. MJ rode the bus to school, so I only had to drop off Sofia. When I returned, Aunt Maddy was still in the kitchen, but she'd showered and dressed and was drinking coffee and reading the newspaper. When she saw me, she set the paper aside.

"I'm guessing from your mood you really did sleep alone last night."

"I've been sleeping alone since I broke up with Daniel," I replied, then popped a coffee pod into the Keurig and waited for it to brew. "But that's not why I'm in a bad mood. And no, I can't tell you anymore so don't ask."

All I'd told her yesterday was I was meeting Alex and I wouldn't be home until late. I'd wanted to tell her everything, but Agent Diaz's admonition rang in my head. *The less she knows the better, for her own safety.*

Aunt Maddy sighed. "Promise me you're being careful."

"I am," I said and joined her at the table with my coffee. "And if it makes you feel any better, apparently Alex's part in all this is to keep me from getting myself killed."

"That does make me feel better."

"Really?" I didn't think she was a fan of Alex since she usually referred to him as the drug dealer unless the kids were around.

"He's a survivor."

I nodded. Whatever else you could say about Alex, that

much was true. "I'm going to have to start spending more time in LA. Probably a few nights a week."

That was the compromise I'd reached with Igor. I'd split my time between LA and Santa Veneta until summer. Once the school year ended, I'd move back to LA full-time. I would just have to find whatever evidence there was to find before then.

"What about the kids?" she asked.

I'd thought about this on the drive home last night. "MJ's pretty self-sufficient. It's really only Sofia we need to worry about. I was thinking we could hire a nanny. I'll pay," I added. That was the one bright spot in all this—my new income. It's not true crime doesn't pay. In my limited experience it paid quite well. When I asked Agent Diaz if I could keep the legal fees Igor would be paying me he told me I could. "As long as they're for actual legal services you provided, then there's no reason you shouldn't."

"We don't need a nanny," Aunt Maddy said. "Sofia's in school every day until two."

"Then a babysitter after school on the days I'm not here." I didn't yet know what my schedule was going to look like. I hadn't even met Mischa yet, although I didn't think he had any more say in this arrangement than I did. Ostensibly, it was Mischa's business, but Igor was funding it and presumably making all the major decisions.

"Let's wait and see if we need one," she said.

I shrugged. "If that's what you want."

We sipped our coffee in silence until she said, "May I ask what you'll be doing when you're in LA?"

"You can ask, but I can't answer." I was starting to feel like Jake.

. . .

I DROVE down to LA Friday morning to meet Mischa. He had chosen the restaurant and he and Alex were already seated at a table when I arrived. I would've preferred to meet Mischa on my own, but Agent Diaz insisted Alex be there too.

Alex pointed me out to Mischa as I approached their table and Mischa stood up. I would never have recognized him as Igor's son. His hair was blond, although based on his dark roots, not his natural color, his jeans and patterned shirt hung loosely on his thin frame, and plenty of women would pay good money to have his full lips and chiseled cheekbones.

I offered Mischa my hand to shake but he ignored it and kissed me on both cheeks. My first thought was maybe he'd grown up in Europe, but when he spoke he had no accent. Alex greeted me with his usual nod, and I reciprocated.

Mischa ordered a bottle of water for the table then opened his menu. "I gather my father hired you to keep me from doing anything stupid," he said without looking up.

I set my menu down. "I don't—"

"It's okay," Mischa said. "You're not the first. Although you're a lot prettier than the last guy."

I didn't know how to respond so I smiled and returned my attention to the menu.

I agreed to split several dishes with Mischa—seaweed salad, lobster tacos, shrimp tempura, and quinoa croquettes—and he ordered for us both. Alex ordered a steak for himself.

We each pulled a square of flat bread from the basket the waiter had left in the center of the table and Mischa asked, "Do you know much about art?"

"Not really," I replied. "But I did work on a couple of big IP cases at Simpson & Scott."

"Am I supposed to know what that means?" Mischa asked.

I smiled. "Intellectual property cases. I'm a lawyer. I used to work for Simpson & Scott, a big law firm downtown."

Mischa nodded. "Ah, I get it now."

"Get what?" I asked.

"The reason my father hired you. He loves to hire 'high class professionals,'" he said with the air quotes. "No disrespect. I'm sure you're very good at whatever it is you do."

"Um, thanks," I said, unsure of the appropriate response.

"It's a growing up poor thing," Mischa continued. "Didn't he tell you the story? He loves telling that story. I must've heard it a thousand times."

I shook my head.

Mischa topped off my water glass and his and leaned in. "My father grew up in a small town outside of Saint Petersburg, which was called Leningrad back then. My father's father worked on a chicken farm and one day my grandfather and the owner of the chicken farm got into a fight. This part of the story varies. Sometimes they fought over a woman, sometimes a bottle of vodka, and sometimes my father claims the owner of the chicken farm owed my grandfather money. However the argument started, it always ends the same. The owner of the chicken farm picked up one of the axes they used to cut the heads off the chickens and threw it at my grandfather. It didn't decapitate him, but it did hit an artery and he bled to death.

"As the story goes, my father, who was somewhere between twelve and fourteen at the time, that part changes too, vowed to avenge my grandfather's death. He followed the owner around the small town for weeks until one night, when the man staggered out of his favorite pub blind drunk, my father strangled him to death with his bare hands. Then, because he didn't want to get sent to the Gulag, my father fled the country and eventually made his way to the United States where he became a very successful businessman. And now people who would've spit on my father if they saw him in the street are on his payroll."

"I would never spit on your father in the street," I said.

"I believe you," Mischa said. "But you are on his payroll."

The thought made my stomach roil, but I couldn't deny it was true, as much as I wanted to. *Forgive me, Jonah.*

Mischa dipped a corner of his bread into the fragrant olive oil and said, "I'm shocked he never told you that story."

"Maybe he will. I just met him a few days ago."

Mischa's eyes widened. "Really?"

"I recommended her," Alex explained.

Mischa looked from Alex to me with a devilish grin. "And how did you two meet?"

Chapter 7

I TOLD Mischa the same story I'd told his father, word for word in case they compared notes.

"Fascinating," Mischa said as he dug into our shared seaweed salad. "Although I guess if you hadn't met that way, you two could've just hooked up on Tinder."

I choked on my shrimp tempura. "Excuse me?"

"You're together, aren't you?" Mischa asked, glancing from me to Alex and back to me again. I could see a smile forming on Alex's lips, but he kept his mouth shut.

"No," I croaked then gulped down half the water in my glass. "Our relationship is purely professional." This wasn't strictly true but to say we were friends wasn't accurate either.

"Oh," Mischa said, "my mistake."

After lunch I drove the three of us to Mischa's gallery, which was only a few blocks away. Mischa and Alex had walked to the restaurant since it was so close. There were two cars in the gallery's parking lot—Alex's black BMW and an orange Lamborghini, which I assumed belonged to Mischa. I wondered if the ostentatious car was another growing up poor thing.

Mischa gave me a tour of the gallery while Alex trailed

behind us. It was a cavernous space with high ceilings, polished cement floors, bright white walls filled with large abstract paintings, and the occasional metal sculpture on a tall wooden table. Then Mischa led me into a windowless back room with a large wood desk, a small black sofa, three tall gunmetal grey filing cabinets, and a red, black, and tan oriental rug covering most of the floor.

"The desk is yours," Mischa said. "I like to be in the gallery where the action is."

There wasn't much action in the gallery today. The place was empty.

"Showings are by appointment only," Mischa continued, as if reading my mind. "Except for opening night exhibitions and those are by invitation. The next one's tomorrow. You should come seeing as how you're working here now."

Was I working in the gallery? Igor had been vague on that point. "What type of work will I be doing exactly?"

Mischa shrugged. "I've no idea. Ask my father. He'll be here tomorrow night too."

I turned to Alex, who had been silent since we'd arrived. "Sorry," he said, "I don't get involved in the high-class, professional side of the business."

I gave him a hard stare but said nothing.

Mischa opened the top desk drawer and pulled out a key ring with one silver key, which he handed to me, then said, "Sixty-nine, fifty-eight, forty-three."

"Excuse me?" I replied.

"The security code," Mischa said. "But you need the key too, so don't lose it. Any questions?"

"Um."

But he was already walking away. "I'll see you tomorrow night," he called out from the hallway. "Cocktail attire. That goes for you too, Alex."

Then I heard the back door slam shut, two beeps, which I assumed was the alarm being re-activated, and Alex and I were alone. I repeated the alarm code several times until I found a pad and pen in the desk. But as soon as I'd written the code down, Alex ripped the paper off the pad and tore it up into tiny pieces, which he stuffed into the front pocket of his black jeans.

"Never write down passcodes," Alex said.

"I know, but I haven't committed it to memory yet."

"Sure, you have." Then before I knew what was happening Alex pulled a gun out from behind his back and pointed it at me. "What's the passcode?"

"What the fuck are you doing?" I screamed.

Alex took a step closer, so the gun was just inches away from me. "Tell me the passcode," he said calmly.

I blurted out the numbers without thinking.

Alex returned the gun to its hiding place while I collapsed onto the desk chair, my heart pounding in my chest. "I told ya you knew it."

"Don't ever, ever, ever do that to me again." It wasn't the first time I'd seen a gun up close. Jake used to carry a gun. But it was the first time anyone had ever pointed one at me. Was the barrel of a gun the last thing Jonah had seen before he died? He must've seen the gun since he was shot from the front, not from behind. I shuddered involuntarily. Jonah must've been terrified. Amelia, thank God, would've been too young to realize what was happening.

"Sorry," Alex said.

"I'm serious, Alex. You could've given me a heart attack. And how the hell are you walking around with a gun?" Even if he owned it legally, which I doubted, he could never have gotten a concealed carry permit in California.

He stared at me as if I was an idiot for even asking the question.

Was that why he always wore the leather jacket, even when the weather was warm? Was it to keep the gun hidden from view? "Do you all carry guns?" I asked. "Did Mischa have one too?"

Alex shook his head. "Not Mischa, but Igor always has one within reach."

"Then should I get one?" I'd have to learn how to shoot, but how hard could that be? There was a new school shooting almost every day.

"No," Alex replied.

"Why not?"

"You should only have a gun if you're prepared to use it."

The drive home on Friday afternoon took three and a half hours. Then I spent another two and half hours driving back on Saturday for the art exhibition. That's when I decided it was time to rent an apartment in LA.

Chapter 8

"I HAVE PLACE FOR YOU," Igor said while we sipped champagne and stared at a giant canvas containing swirls of pink and purple paint on a dark blue background. The price was eight thousand dollars and it was already sold. "Nice apartment," he continued. "High floor. Beautiful view."

I'd been trying to avoid Igor, but no matter where I went in the gallery, he seemed to appear at my side. If his wife was there too, I didn't know where she was. He never introduced us or even mentioned her name. Mischa chatted with me too, but his presence didn't bother me. I felt sorry for him. I'd been watching his interactions with his father all evening and it was clearly not a loving relationship. Whenever Igor spoke to Mischa, which wasn't often, he barked orders at him like he did to Sergey. And as far as I knew, Mischa had nothing to do with Jonah and Amelia's murder.

I wouldn't have minded being Mischa's beard, but he showed no interest in me. I wondered if he thought his father had hired me to spy on him. He would be partially right. I was there to spy on him, but it was on behalf of the FBI.

"I could show you the apartment now," Igor said. "It's not far from here."

I wasn't sure if this was a come-on or a legitimate offer. Was Igor tired of screwing teenagers and wanted someone a little older? Or maybe he just wanted to fuck one of his "high class professionals." Either way, the thought of him touching me made my skin crawl. I glanced around for Alex, but I didn't see him, so I said the first excuse that came to my mind. "Sorry, I'm afraid of heights." I wasn't, but Igor didn't know that.

"Then I'll find you apartment on lower floor."

I shook my head. "Thank you for the offer but I'm looking for a house with a yard. I like to garden." I had no interest in gardening, but Igor didn't know that either.

Igor nodded. "Yes. You should get house with pool. For the kids."

My hope was the kids would never visit me in LA, but I didn't share that sentiment with Igor. I was just glad he didn't offer me a house with a pool too.

"How was the party?" my aunt asked when I stumbled into the kitchen the next morning. I wasn't hungover—I'd only drank one glass of champagne—but I was exhausted. There had been an accident on the freeway last night, and my drive home had taken almost four hours.

"Was it a birthday party?" Sofia asked as she squeezed half a bottle of syrup onto her pancakes. She'd been invited to two birthday parties in the past month and was now obsessed with them. She wanted to start planning her own party even though her birthday wasn't for another four months.

"No," I said, popping a coffee pod into the Keurig. "It was a party for an artist who was showing his paintings at a gallery."

"Can I show my pictures at a gallery and get a party too?"

I smiled and followed her gaze to her crayon drawings, which covered the fridge. They were good for her age, I thought, but I didn't think she'd be selling her artwork for eight thousand dollars a pop anytime soon. "When you're a grownup, sure. You're very talented. Do you want me to buy you some paints so you can make paintings too?"

"Yes!" Sofia said and went back to her pancakes.

I turned to Aunt Maddy, who gave me an arched eyebrow as she flipped the last two pancakes. I knew she was worried about the mess. "Washable paints," I said. "We can set up an easel in the backyard."

"Was Uncle Alex there too?" MJ asked as I sat down at the table with my coffee.

"Yes," I replied. "Why do you ask?"

He shrugged. "I dunno." Then he stuffed half a pancake into his mouth.

My aunt joined us at the kitchen table with the last two pancakes. She and I each took one, but she covered hers with syrup and I covered mine with fresh strawberries.

"I didn't know Alex was going to be there too," my aunt said, cutting her pancake with the side of her fork.

My mouth was full, so I used that as an excuse not to reply.

Aunt Maddy waited until the kids finished eating and left the table before she questioned me further. "Why was Alex at an art opening? It doesn't really seem like his kind of thing."

"It's not really my kind of thing either."

"Is he your bodyguard now?"

"Do you see him here?" I asked.

She pursed her lips and stared at me.

"Sorry," I said, "but you know I can't tell you anything, so please stop asking."

"You should know I'm not the only one asking questions." Then she picked up her and Sofia's dirty plates and carried them to the sink. "Your absence has not gone unnoticed, especially by MJ."

I sighed and took another sip of my coffee. This was going to be harder than I thought.

I found MJ in the living room playing a car game on his Xbox, a Christmas present from Alex.

"Can we talk for a sec?" I asked.

"Sure," he said, "let me finish this race." A minute later he set the controller down. "What's up?"

"I know I've been gone a lot lately and I just wanted you to know it's because I have a new client in LA. He has a lot of work for me, and I thought it might be easier if I rented a place down there for a few months, so I don't have to keep driving back and forth all the time. But nothing changes for you and Sofia. You're both going to still live here with Aunt Maddy, and I'll be here on the weekends and at least a couple of nights during the week."

"Who's your new client?" he asked.

"Just some businessman your uncle introduced me to."

A wave of concern crossed his face. "My uncle knows some pretty bad dudes."

"It's all good," I said without hesitation. "Nothing for you to worry about. Okay?"

"Okay," he said unconvincingly.

I stood up to leave and he picked up the controller again. As I climbed the stairs to my bedroom it struck me that my lying to MJ was really no different than all the lies Jake and Jonah had told me. I hadn't spoken to Jake in months. I still hadn't forgiven him for the part he played in Jonah and Amelia's deaths, but I was starting to understand.

. . .

I WAS in my office Monday afternoon when the bell on the front door tinkled. I was drafting a status report in Olivia Baylor's custody dispute. This was my last remaining case from my partnership with Janelle. She had taken the rest of the clients with her when she moved to her new law firm, but I kept the Baylor case because Olivia insisted she was tired of lawyers and I was the only one she would talk to.

"I'll be right there," I called out then saved and closed my document. Since MJ had joined the basketball team at the Winston Academy, I no longer had a receptionist. The team practiced three afternoons a week, and the other two afternoons he tutored Olivia and another student in math. I missed MJ's company, but I was happy he'd settled in at his new school. Since he'd started seeing a therapist once a week, someone Dr. Rubenstein had recommended, he hadn't had any more outbursts on campus and he seemed happier all around.

My visitor didn't respond, which didn't surprise me. The UPS man never responded when I called out to him either. He just dropped the package on the floor inside the door and left. It wasn't until I stepped out into the reception area that I panicked.

Chapter 9

"Igor, what are you doing here?" It wasn't just Igor; he'd brought Sergey with him too. Sergey was sitting on the couch scanning his phone. Igor was standing with his back to me, staring out the front window at Mike Murphy's auto repair shop across the street.

Sergey ignored me. Igor turned around. "I wanted to see this office you refuse to leave."

He didn't look impressed. I couldn't blame him. My office looked like what it was—a cheap strip mall space. He would've liked my office at Simpson & Scott much better. It was on the eighteenth floor of a high rise building in downtown LA.

"It's not the office that's keeping me in Santa Veneta," I said, which he already knew. It made me wonder why he'd driven up from LA. Was he trying to intimidate me?

Igor didn't respond, but continued to stare at me.

I licked my lips and breathed deeply in an attempt to slow my heart rate. When I knew in advance I'd be seeing Igor I could prepare myself. But his showing up in Santa Veneta unannounced was messing with my head, which was likely his intent. "Can I get you something to drink?" I asked. "Coffee? Water?"

He shook his head. "I came to talk to you."

"You didn't need to drive all the way up here just to talk to me. That's what phones are for. Or video conferences, if you prefer."

"We talk in person. Safer that way."

I wasn't sure why he thought an in-person conversation was safer. If he was concerned about our conversation being recorded, it could just as easily be recorded in-person too. But I said, "Of course. Let's go to my office."

Sergey finally looked up from his phone, but he remained seated on the couch in the reception area while Igor followed me. Igor sat down heavily in one of my office guest chairs and I took the seat behind my desk. "What did you want to discuss?"

"I need you to set up ten companies."

I reached for my pen and a blank legal pad. "Sure. Have you decided on corporate structure yet? Corporation? Partnership? LLC? There are pros and cons to each."

"We'll get to that later. Each of these companies is going to hire you."

"Hire me to do what?" I asked.

"Provide legal services."

"I assumed. Can you be more specific?"

He waved away my question. "You will send each of these companies a retainer agreement for ten thousand dollars each. The money will be wired to you, and when it's gone, the retainers will be replenished. I will direct you how to spend the funds. Do you understand?"

I stared across the desk at Igor. Yes, I understood. He wanted me to use my client trust account to launder his dirty money. If these companies deposited money into the bank, the bank would be obligated to question the source of the funds and report any suspicious activity to the government. But a lawyer depositing funds into a pooled client trust account had no such obligation.

I realized this was the purpose of Igor's unannounced visit today—to lay out the scheme and see whether I was willing to go along with it. "Yes," I said.

"Good." Igor stood up. "I'll meet you at the gallery tomorrow morning at ten."

I agreed, mentally calculating I'd need to leave the house by seven to allow time for traffic, which I was sure to hit somewhere along the way.

I ENDED up leaving the house at six a.m. because Agent Diaz wanted to meet with me and Alex before I met with Igor at the gallery. We rendezvoused in a grocery store parking lot again, but a different grocery store than the last time. Today we had three cars since we'd all driven separately, so Alex and I slid into the backseat of Agent Diaz's car. As soon as I'd shut the door, Agent Diaz handed me a shopping bag. I peeked inside and saw a package of legal pads, a box of pens, and an I Heart LA coffee mug.

I reached for the coffee mug first. "Is this supposed to be a joke?"

"Use it as a pencil cup," Agent Diaz said. "If anyone asks, you can tell them it was a gift from Alex."

I turned to Alex, who looked like he'd just woken up. His black clothes were wrinkled and his face was covered with stubble. Obviously he hadn't bothered to shave this morning. "I can't really see you buying me this, can you?"

"No," he yawned.

Agent Diaz sighed, then took the cup from my hand and tossed it onto the passenger seat. "If you don't like mine, go buy one of your own. It's the pen that's important." Then he reached into the bag and pulled out a pen that was lying loose at the bottom. "It's a recording device."

I took the pen from him and examined it. "Really? It looks like a regular pen."

"That's the point. It's a regular pen too. You can write with it. In fact, you should write with it, so no one will suspect anything if they see it sitting on your desk. It's voice activated."

Agent Diaz showed me how to turn it on and off and I tested it out with the three of us. It recorded our conversation perfectly. "This is so cool!" I knew recording pens existed, but I'd never used one before. Although I liked the novelty of it, they seemed unnecessary these days since anyone could record anything they wanted on their phone. When I pointed that out to Agent Diaz, he admonished me.

"You are not under any circumstances to attempt to record Igor or any of his men with your phone."

"Why not?" I asked.

Alex answered for him. "Because if they notice, they will kill you."

"Do you think Igor's suspicious of me?" I hadn't gotten that vibe from him at the gallery Saturday night or when he came to my office yesterday.

"Igor's suspicious of everyone," Alex replied.

"You don't grow old in his line of work by trusting people," Agent Diaz added.

"So, my phone is suspicious but my pen's not?"

Agent Diaz pulled the box of pens out of the bag. They were the same black and silver design as the recording pen. "Not when you have a handful of them sitting on your desk and you write with them all the time. They'll fade into the background, which is why you need a pencil cup."

I nodded. "Understood. Once the pen records, how do I

download the recording? Or am I uploading it?" The tech side was the part that always tripped me up.

"You won't be doing either," Agent Diaz said. "You have a briefcase, right?"

"Yes," I replied.

"When you pack up your stuff at the end of the day, toss a pen into your briefcase with whatever else you normally take home with you. But leave the recording pen on your desk so it can record when you're not there. Every few days Alex will give you another one and then you can swap them out."

"What if I hear something important? Should I call him to pick it up sooner?"

"No," Agent Diaz said. "Just stick to the plan."

"Do you want me to listen to it in the mornings when I arrive? Obviously, I would only do that if was alone."

"No, I want you to ignore the pen unless you happen to be writing with it. If it records anything pertinent, I'll let you know. Any more questions?"

I STOPPED at Staples on my way to the gallery and bought a pencil cup, along with an assortment of colored pens, a package of highlighters, and a stapler. I arrived at the gallery five minutes before ten and Igor and Sergey were already sitting in the parking lot in Igor's black Mercedes, Sergey behind the wheel and Igor in the back seat. I parked two spaces down from them, and they both got out of the car.

"What's in the bag?" Igor asked as he and Sergey followed me to the front door.

"Office supplies," I said, thankful I'd had the presence of mind to replace one of the pens in the box with the recorder pen before I left the Staples parking lot.

"We don't have office supplies?" Igor asked, watching me punch in the security code.

"I don't know what you have," I replied as I unlocked the front door. "But I'm particular about my pens and paper. Don't worry, I won't charge you for them."

Igor chuckled and he and Sergey followed me through the gallery to the windowless office in the back. I dropped my shopping bag and purse on the desk and slid my briefcase underneath. Igor sat down in the center of the sofa, which was really the size of a love seat, and spread his arms and legs wide. I was trying to figure out where Sergey was going to sit when Igor told him he could wait outside. Sergey closed the office door behind him, leaving me and Igor alone.

Chapter 10

I HUNG my suit jacket on the back of my chair and pulled the recording pen and a blank legal pad out of the shopping bag. "Did you decide which corporate structure you want for the companies?" I asked, not looking up from my desk. Maybe if I didn't have to see Igor, I could better control my emotions. It was taking all my willpower not to walk over to the sofa and stab him in the side of the neck with the recording pen. Although I didn't know if you could break the skin with just a pen, even one with a recorder inside. I should've purchased a letter opener too.

Igor shook his head. "All business with you. No sweet talk."

I looked up at Igor, who now had his arms folded across his chest. There was no way I could take him down physically. He'd break my arm before I ever got the pen close to his carotid artery. I dropped the pen onto the blank pad and clasped my hands in front of me. "I bill by tenths of an hour. But it's your money. How are you this morning, Igor? Did you hit much traffic driving home yesterday?"

Igor let out a raucous laugh. "Sergey's good driver. Always finds fastest route. But next time I visit, I'll leave later and miss traffic. We'll have dinner and you can show me around city you love so much."

I was sorry to hear there was going to be a next time. I was hoping now that Igor had seen my office, he'd never visit Santa Veneta again. "If you're planning on coming up to Santa Veneta regularly, then maybe I don't need to move to LA after all."

"No," he said. "I need you here."

"Why? Everything I'll be doing for you can be handled by phone or email." Which was definitely my preference. Sometimes when we were just talking business, I could forget what he did to my family and pretend he was a regular client.

"No, we talk in person only. Understand?"

Yes, I understood. He didn't want anything that could be printed, copied, or recorded. Although I was recording this conversation now. But Igor didn't know that. And he'd yet to say anything incriminating. "You realize by setting up all these companies, I'll be leaving a paper trail. There's no way around it."

"Of course, of course. Everything by the book. All legal."

The *appearance* of legal. "I can do that."

"Yes," he said. "That's why I hire you. So when are you moving?"

"I'm not sure. I need to find a place first."

"I told you, I have beautiful apartment. Very close to here."

And would he be letting himself into my beautiful apartment whenever he wanted? Or was it outfitted with hidden cameras so he could keep tabs on me? "I appreciate the offer, but I'm going to take your suggestion." He couldn't disagree if it was his suggestion. "I'm going to rent a house with a pool for the kids."

"Yes, good idea. But move soon." Then he got up from the couch and opened the office door. I thought he was leaving, but he only called out to Sergey. A minute later Sergey appeared with a stack of manila file folders, which he dropped onto my desk. "The information you need is there," Igor said.

I didn't know where the files had come from. Sergey didn't have them when we all walked in together this morning. Had they been in Igor's car? Were they hidden somewhere else in the building? I forced myself to smile and said, "Great. When I'm done with these, do you want me to lock them in the file cabinet?"

I nodded to the three tall file cabinets lined up like soldiers along one wall. They each contained a lock in the upper right-hand corner. Mischa hadn't given me a key to the file cabinets, but I was hoping Igor would. No sense keeping secrets from your lawyer. I was dying to search those cabinets for incriminating evidence. If I could find something quickly, maybe I wouldn't have to move to LA even temporarily.

"No," Igor said. "Give them back to Sergey. He'll wait."

I nodded to the tall stack of files. "Igor, it's going to take me a while to go through all of these."

"It's okay," Igor replied. "Sergey's not in rush. Right, Sergey?"

"*Da*," Sergey said.

"See," Igor said. "All fine. I see you back here tomorrow, same time."

The click-clack of Igor's shoes on the cement floor echoed through the empty gallery. Then I heard the alarm beep twice and I knew he was gone. I thought Sergey would disappear to wherever he'd been when Igor and I were talking, but instead, he took Igor's place on the sofa. "You work now," he said, then he placed earbuds in his ears and closed his eyes.

It was hard enough trying to make sense of the byzantine structure of Igor's existing legal entities without having Sergey sitting six feet away from me too, but I did my best to ignore him. When he hadn't moved in a while, I thought maybe he'd fallen asleep. He hadn't. The first time I stood up from the desk, he opened his eyes.

"Bathroom?" I asked.

He nodded toward the back of the building. "End of hall."

"Thanks," I said and reached inside the desk for my purse.

"Leave it. I won't steal anything."

I forced a smile. "I didn't think you would."

Sergey didn't smile back. "Leave the bag."

I slid my purse onto my shoulder. "No, I need it."

Sergey pulled the earbuds out of his ears and stood up. "Why?"

"Haven't you ever been out to dinner with a woman? We always take our purses to the ladies room."

Sergey closed the space between us and ripped the bag from my shoulder.

"What the fuck!"

Sergey ignored me as he unzipped the top of my purse, turned it upside down, and dumped the contents onto my desk. Then he stuck his hand inside the bag and felt around. He was only pawing my purse, not me, but I still felt violated. Maybe it was the smirk on his face.

"Give that back," I yelled. I reached for the bag and Sergey pushed me so hard I stumbled backward into one of the file cabinets. The corner of the metal cabinet was sharp and it dug into my back. I yelped but Sergey couldn't have cared less. I reached over my shoulder and felt the tear in my shirt. My skin wasn't wet, so I assumed I wasn't bleeding, but I was definitely bruised. "What the hell is wrong with you?"

Sergey pulled the tampon package, which had been zipped inside an inner compartment, out of my purse and held it up, triumphant. "Is this what you need?"

"None of your fucking business," I said as my eyes filled

with tears, as much from the pain in my back as his vile behavior.

Sergey licked his lips. "I'll help. I slide it right in. Move it around, like this." He demonstrated with his groin. "Is that what you like?"

I didn't answer him, but my heart was pounding so loud he must've heard it too. I wanted to run, but Sergey was standing between me and the door and that was the only exit. Sergey was acting like an animal, so I tried to remember what you were supposed to do if you happened upon a bear in the woods. Were you supposed to stand perfectly still and hope the bear lost interest? Or were you supposed to make a lot of noise and hope the bear slinked away? Or were those the instructions for what to do if you encountered a snake?

The last time I felt cornered was with Daniel. The situation wasn't the same; I never feared Daniel would attack me. But what I'd done that night had worked. I stood up straight and said, "Get the fuck out my office before I call Igor. I don't think he's going to be too pleased with your behavior."

Sergey smirked. "I'm best bodyguard he ever had."

"You sure about that? If you're such a great bodyguard, then why did he leave you here with me? Who's with him now?"

Sergey stopped smirking and threw the tampon at me. I was so startled that instead of catching it, it bounced off my chest and landed on the floor. "Be quick," he said. "You have work to do." Then he went back to the sofa.

I grabbed my keys and phone from the pile of stuff on my desk and sprinted for the door. As soon as I opened it, the alarm blared, but I didn't stop. I ran to my car then squealed out of the parking lot. I didn't have a destination in mind; I just wanted to get away from Sergey. But I was shaking so badly it was hard to drive. As soon as I saw an open parking space I pulled over.

Even if Sergey followed me, which I doubted, I didn't think he'd attack me in the middle of Sunset Boulevard.

I reached for my phone and called Agent Diaz. My call went straight to his voicemail, and I hung up without leaving a message. Next, I called Alex. He picked up on the second ring.

"I need your help," I said.

"What happened?" he asked.

"Sergey," I said and gulped air. Obviously, I was breathing, but it didn't feel that way.

"Where are you? At the gallery?"

"No, but I'm still in Hollywood." I glanced out the windshield. "A couple of blocks from the Rock & Roll Ralphs." That wasn't the store's actual name, it's just what everyone called it because it was close to the clubs and was busy late at night after the bars closed.

"Wait there. I'll come to you."

"Okay, but can you stay on the phone with me?" I was shaking less now, but still shaking.

"Sure," he said and his voice softened. "What's up with the kids? Is MJ dating that Olivia girl yet?"

Chapter 11

Talking about the kids helped. It got my mind off Sergey. By the time Alex told me he was pulling into the Rock & Roll Ralphs parking lot, I'd stopped shaking and was able to drive the three blocks to meet him there. I spotted his black BMW in the first aisle, and I pulled into the closest open space. Alex appeared next to the driver's side window before I'd even shut off the engine. As soon as I pushed the button to unlock my doors, he opened mine.

He scanned my body, looking for injuries I supposed, then returned to my face. "What happened?"

I started crying again, part residual fear and part embarrassment as I realized that Sergey hadn't actually done anything besides frighten me. I gave Alex an abbreviated version of events, then said, "I overreacted. I never should've run. Now I've ruined everything."

He shook his head. "You haven't."

"I set off the goddamn burglar alarm, Alex. What if the police came? You think Igor's going to be happy with me? You don't think he's going to fire me for this? I'm probably already fired." I dropped my head in my hands and started bawling. How could I screw this up so badly? And on my first day!

Alex grabbed me by my shoulders and I winced. He pulled his hands back, confused. "I thought he didn't—"

"He didn't," I said, looking up. "I fell into a file cabinet."

"No one falls into a file cabinet."

"He pushed me. It's just bruised."

"Let me see it," Alex said.

"No, it's fine. I'll be fine."

"Turn around, Grace."

I closed my eyes and pivoted in my seat. I felt Alex's fingers brush the tear in my shirt, but he didn't touch my skin. "You should go home and put some ice on it. I'll talk to Igor."

I sniffed loudly and wiped my eyes. "Thanks, but I don't think I'm up for a two-hour-plus drive right now."

"Then come to my house."

"Your house?"

"I have a home too. Or did you think I lived in the street?"

"No, I just—"

"Give me your phone."

"What?"

Alex reached across me and pulled my phone out of the cup holder. He held it up to my face and it opened, then he started tapping the screen.

"What are you—"

"Directions," he said and handed it back to me. I looked down and saw he'd opened the Waze app. "Let's get started," the chipper Waze voice announced.

"Are you okay to drive?" Alex asked.

I nodded.

"Okay. I'll meet you at my place."

I tried to follow Alex but I lost him on the freeway. I recognized his car in the driveway when I pulled up in front of a small, well-kept house in a neighborhood I'd never been to before despite its proximity to my alma mater.

During law school I'd shared an apartment with one of my classmates on the Westside of the city. After graduation Jonah and I rented a place together in Los Feliz because it was closer to both our offices. On the weekends we drove everywhere, occasionally venturing north to visit my aunt in Santa Veneta, south for an overnight in San Diego, and east to visit friends in Pasadena. But in all the years I'd lived in Southern California, I'd never been to Boyle Heights before today.

I told this to Alex, who was sitting on the steps of his front porch.

"Did you think that would surprise me?" he said as he stood up and unlocked his front door.

"I guess not." Boyle Heights was one of LA's oldest neighborhoods. Over the past hundred and fifty years it had been home to a multitude of immigrant populations. These days it was almost exclusively Latino. I was probably the only person in the neighborhood who didn't speak Spanish fluently.

Alex's house was a quintessential California bungalow—hardwood floors, low ceilings, and dark wood trim. He led me through the living room, which was clean and clutter free, and down a short hall to the back of the house, which contained two bedrooms with a bathroom in between.

"You can lie down if you want," Alex said, pointing to the bedroom on the right. "I'll get you some ice for your back."

I wandered into the room, taking in the burgundy bedspread, the armchair with the doilies, and the giant ceramic Jesus attached to a wooden cross on the wall above the bed.

Alex returned with a bag of ice wrapped in a kitchen towel.

"I didn't know you were so religious," I said, nodding to the cross.

Alex cracked a smile. "This was my mother's room. This was her house."

"And now you live here?"

"I've always lived here. I'll be down the hall if you need me." He closed the bedroom door on his way out.

I walked over to the dresser, which was covered with framed photos. There were a bunch of MJ and Sofia when they were younger and a few of Alex and Maria too. There were also two large wedding photos—an old black and white one, which I assumed from the vintage was a picture of Alex's grandparents, and another that appeared to be from the seventies based on the groom's pale blue tuxedo with matching bowtie and ruffled tuxedo shirt. *That must be his parents.* Minus the clothes and the mustache, Alex looked exactly like his father.

I sat down on the edge of the bed and held the ice pack to my bruised shoulder then decided I'd be more comfortable if I laid down. I moved to my stomach, carefully balancing the ice pack on my back, and breathed in. The bed smelled musty, like an old person's home. I thought the scent would keep me awake, but it didn't. I drifted off to sleep almost immediately but jolted awake from a bad dream. I couldn't remember any details, but I remembered Sergey was in it.

I picked up the bag of ice, which had slid onto the floor, and carried it into the bathroom. I dumped the half-melted cubes into the sink and hung the moist towel over the shower rod. I could hear Alex talking to someone, and since his was the only voice I heard, I assumed he was on the phone. I didn't want to disturb him, so I decided to stay in the back of the house.

I stepped out into the hallway and stared at the two bedrooms. To my right was Alex's mother's room and to my left was the room I presumed was Alex's bedroom. I knew which room I *should* go to, but I walked in the opposite direction instead.

Chapter 12

The walls were not adorned with posters of half-naked women and there were no textbooks sitting on the student-sized desk, but I imagined this room looked much the same as it did when Alex was a teenager. There was an old, wooden, six-drawer dresser and a double bed with a plain navy quilt pushed up against one wall. On the opposite wall was a closet with sliding wood doors.

I suddenly remembered Dr. Rubenstein's reaction when I'd first told her about Alex and I smiled. When I'd proclaimed that his entire wardrobe was black, she'd asked me if I'd seen inside his closet. At the time I thought I never would. *Now's your chance.*

I listened for a moment and could still hear him talking, so I took a step toward the closet. The floor squeaked beneath me, and I froze. I half expected Alex to come running down the hall, gun in hand. I stood where I was and waited until I heard his voice again, then I continued.

I slid open the door on the left side first. There were double bars, but the closet wasn't stuffed. The top bar held mostly T-shirts, but a few sweatshirts and a couple of long-sleeved button-downs too. Jeans and two pairs of pants hung on the bottom bar. His clothes weren't *all* black, but close. I reached for the door to slide it closed when I heard his voice behind me. "What are you doing?"

I spun around. Alex was standing in the doorway to his bedroom, his arms folded across his chest and his lips pursed.

"I, um." I quickly turned and pulled the closet door closed, then faced Alex again. "I heard you on the phone and I didn't want to bother you."

"So, you thought you'd snoop through my things instead."

"I wasn't snooping. I was just looking."

He placed his hands on his hips. "I guess I'm just a dumb high school dropout because I always thought they were the same. And snooping in this neighborhood can get you shot."

"You're right. I'm sorry. I had no right to invade your privacy. I apologize."

"Did you find what you were looking for?"

"I wasn't looking for anything."

His dark eyes bore into me.

"Honest," I said. "The whole thing's ridiculous. If I told you, you'd laugh."

"Try me," he replied.

I sighed and stared down at the floor, too embarrassed to look at him. "I just wanted to know if you owned any non-black clothing."

"What?"

"I told you it was ridiculous."

"Why do you care what color my clothes are?"

"Because when I told my therapist about you, she said you sounded like a colorful fellow, and I said that wasn't true since your entire wardrobe was black. Then she'd asked if I'd seen inside your closet and knew that for a fact."

Alex cracked a smile. "If you wanted to know so badly, why didn't you just ask me?"

"Because then you would've wanted to know why I was asking, and then I would've had to explain, and that would've prompted more questions, and it just wasn't worth the effort."

"Is your curiosity satisfied now?"

"Actually, I only got to see one side."

Alex sealed his lips together and blew air out of his nose, which I knew meant he was annoyed with me, but he walked over to the closet and slid open the door on the other side. Black boots, black shoes, black Converse high-tops, a pair of Nikes in black, white, and blue, and two non-leather jackets, one black and one army green.

"Thank you. Now I'm satisfied."

He slid the closet door shut. "Don't you want to check my drawers too? You might find some interesting things in there."

"No, I'm good."

He nodded. "Then we can leave."

"Where are we going?"

"Back to the gallery."

"Why?"

"Igor wants to talk to you."

Chapter 13

At the mention of Igor's name my heart started racing. "Is Sergey going to be there too?"

"He didn't say," Alex replied.

Alex started toward his bedroom door, but I stayed rooted to my spot. "I don't think I'm ready to go back yet."

Alex turned and stared at me. "It wasn't a request."

"I know, but if Sergey's there..."

"Sergey's handled."

"How?"

"I spoke to Igor. He thinks you're my woman. Sergey won't touch you now."

Before this morning I would've objected, but now I saw the wisdom in this plan. "And how do we sell it to Igor?"

Alex chuckled. "No selling necessary. He told me to put a ring on it before you changed your mind."

I laughed. "I didn't realize Igor was a Beyoncé fan."

Alex nodded. "Rihanna too. C'mon, let's go."

He motioned for me to leave his bedroom and followed me down the hallway. But when we reached the living room, he told me to wait while he ran back to his bedroom. He returned with his green utility jacket, which he draped around my shoulders. "No woman of mine walks around with a hole in her shirt."

I wanted to drive myself to the gallery because I planned on returning to Santa Veneta right after the meeting, but Alex thought it would be better if we arrived together since that's what a couple would do. When we entered the gallery I was glad I'd taken Alex's advice because Sergey was standing at Igor's side.

Alex placed his arm around my shoulder, careful not to touch my bruise, and whispered in my ear, "Let me handle this."

I nodded and kept walking. We stopped a few feet from Igor and Sergey, next to a tall table with a metal sculpture on top. It resembled nothing I could ascertain and I had no idea what it was meant to represent.

Igor spoke first. "I understand we had little misunderstanding earlier."

"A misunderstanding?" I said. "Is that what he told you?"

Alex leaned over and whispered in my ear. "Stop talking."

I pressed my lips together to keep myself from speaking again.

"Not cool, bro," Alex said to Sergey.

"Sorry," Sergey said. "I didn't know."

I shrugged off Alex's arm. "Wait, are you apologizing to him instead of me?"

Igor stepped forward. "He's apologizing to both of you." Then he yelled something at Sergey in Russian.

Sergey turned to me. "I'm sorry for misunderstanding."

"Misunderstanding?" I said, my voice rising. "Is that what we're calling attempted rape these days?"

"There was no attempt," Sergey said. "If I wanted you, I would've taken you."

"You would've taken me?" I said, my voice rising even higher. "Who the fuck do you think I am?"

"Enough!" Igor yelled. Then he spoke to Sergey in Russian again, which from the expression on Sergey's face was not what he wanted to hear. Then Igor turned to me. "Sergey apologized. Now you accept his apology and we're all friends again."

"Friends?" I said.

Alex grabbed me by my upper arm and spun me around, so I was facing him with my back to Igor and Sergey. He didn't have to say it; I knew exactly what he wanted. I pulled away from him and turned back to Sergey. "Apology accepted."

Igor clapped his hands together. "Good. Now we put this behind us and get back to work."

"I'm sorry," I said, "but I need to go home. I'll be back tomorrow and I'll stay as late as I need to finish."

Igor nodded. "Okay. You need mental health day. I understand. Tomorrow Sergey will be on best behavior."

"No," I said. "No more Sergey. I work alone."

Alex pulled his car keys out of his pocket and held them up to me. "Wait for me in the car."

"But—"

Alex lowered his voice and spoke very slowly. "I said, wait for me in the car, Grace."

If it were just the two of us, I would've argued with him, but Igor and Sergey were watching. I was Alex's woman now, or so they thought. Would Alex put up with his woman disrespecting him? I doubted it. And I wasn't sure what he would do if I tried. I didn't like this charade, but I needed to play my part. I grabbed Alex's keys and stomped out of the gallery, not caring that the alarm blared the moment I pushed open the door. One of the macho men inside could turn it off.

Alex joined me in his car a few minutes later.

"So?" I asked as he turned on the engine.

"You and Sergey will not be alone in the gallery, but when you meet with Igor, Sergey will be there too. There's no way around that."

"Thank you," I said.

Alex nodded and pulled out of the parking lot.

"At least one good thing has come out of this," I said.

"What's that?" Alex asked.

"Without Sergey there, I'll be able to do some snooping. I'm dying to get a look inside those file cabinets."

"No," Alex said.

"No?" I replied.

"Igor agreed too easily. He has security cameras in the gallery. He must have them in the office too."

"If he has security cameras in the office, then why did he leave Sergey there to begin with?"

"I don't know. Maybe he was trying to intimidate you. Or maybe he was off to bang his mistress and it was easier to leave Sergey behind. I have no idea. The point is it's not safe for you to go snooping, so don't."

"Then how am I going to get the evidence we need?"

"That's what the recording pen is for."

"A recording's not enough. We need documents. It's the best way to make a case. Documents can't be refuted."

Alex didn't answer me. But the next time we stopped at a red light, he reached for his phone.

"Who are you texting?" I asked.

Chapter 14

ALEX DROVE us to a warehouse complex east of the city. Agent Diaz was waiting for us inside one of the cavernous buildings, which was empty but for a long table and half a dozen, metal, folding chairs. The three of us sat down at one end of the table. "Tell me everything you remember," Agent Diaz said.

When I finished, Alex told Agent Diaz about his phone call with Igor when we were at his house and their subsequent conversation in the gallery after Alex had banished me to the car. I suspected Alex edited some of Igor and Sergey's comments about me.

Agent Diaz did a lot of nodding and scribbling on his notepad.

"Can you make a case with just recordings?" I asked when Alex finished.

"It depends what's on the recordings," Agent Diaz said, "but realistically, probably not. It's unlikely Igor's going to confess to anything."

But when I offered to search the file cabinets Agent Diaz agreed with Alex that it was too risky. "If I'm not allowed to snoop then how are we ever going to get the evidence we need to put him away?"

"It's early days," Agent Diaz said, closing his notepad. "Investigations like these can go on for years sometimes."

"Years? You expect me to work for the man who murdered my family for years?"

Agent Diaz stared at me quizzically. "Grace, this was your idea. You begged me to let you do this."

"Because I wanted you to re-open the investigation. I didn't know I'd be doing this for years."

"I'm not saying it will definitely take years," he said, clicking his pen shut. "It could be a few months. You have to be patient. Let's see where the investigation leads."

Patience was not my strong suit, either in Before or After, apparently.

"Do you think they bought you two as a couple?" Agent Diaz asked Alex.

"Definitely." Alex laughed. "Igor told me to buy her a ring."

Agent Diaz laughed too. "Make sure to invite me to the wedding."

I was the only one who wasn't laughing. "And what happens if Igor finds out we're not a couple?"

"It's your job to make sure he doesn't find out," Agent Diaz said. "Both your jobs."

"But we don't live together," I said. "All he'd have to do is send Sergey to follow one of us home."

Agent Diaz slid his pad and pen into his jacket pocket. "He already knows you live in Santa Veneta."

"But I told him I was renting a house in LA," I replied. "What about the nights I'm in town?"

"She's right," Alex said. "If we're never together, it'll look suspicious."

"Then you stay there too," Agent Diaz said, nodding at Alex. "Separate bedrooms."

"Of course, separate bedrooms," I said.

Neither one of them answered me, but I could feel my cheeks heating up.

WHEN I WALKED into my aunt's house after an almost three-hour drive back from LA, I found her in the kitchen, pulling a roasted chicken out of the oven. I breathed in the scent of onion, rosemary, and sage. "Mmmm. Smells delicious," I said as I dropped down into a kitchen chair.

"Just in time," she replied. "You can uncork the wine."

I purposely hadn't been drinking much lately but I felt like I'd earned a glass of wine after today. I'd just decanted the bottle when I heard footsteps on the stairs and MJ and Sofia appeared in the doorway. Aunt Maddy directed them to set the table, which they did without complaint.

When we were all seated at the dining room table digging into roasted chicken, honey-glazed carrots, and egg noodles, Aunt Maddy asked me, "Are you cold?"

"No," I said, "Why?"

She nodded to Alex's green utility jacket, which I was still wearing. He hadn't asked for it back and I'd forgotten to give it to him, but I couldn't take it off now because if I did, Aunt Maddy would surely notice the tear in my shirt and ask how I'd gotten it.

"I'm comfortable," I said and returned my attention to my food.

"Uncle Alex has a jacket like that," MJ said, and Aunt Maddy's eyebrows shot up.

"I know," I replied. "This is his. He lent it to me."

"You saw my uncle today?" MJ asked at the same time Aunt Maddy said, "Is that so."

I ignored my aunt and responded to MJ. "Yes. I told you my client in LA is someone your uncle introduced me to. We all had a meeting today. The office was cold, and your uncle lent me his jacket."

Sofia said, "You and Uncle Alex work together?"

Maddy and MJ both turned to me. "No, not exactly. But we see each other sometimes."

"When's he coming to visit me?" Sofia asked.

"I don't know," I answered. "Next time I see him I'll ask."

After dinner MJ helped Aunt Maddy clean up while I went upstairs with Sofia to start the bath and bedtime routine. After she fell asleep, I checked on MJ, who was in his room with his laptop open and earbuds in his ears. Then I went to my own room to change clothes. I had just pulled an oversized T-shirt over my head when Aunt Maddy knocked on my bedroom door.

I opened the door and my aunt immediately zeroed in on Alex's jacket, which was laying across the foot of the bed. She reached for it and held it up by one finger as if it was toxic. "Anything you want to tell me?" she asked.

"Nope," I said, "except it's not what you think."

She dropped the jacket back onto the bed. "Then enlighten me."

I sighed. I knew she was not going to let this go. "Remember when I told you Agent Diaz thought it would be safer for me if Igor and his crew thought I was Alex's girlfriend?"

"Yes. But I thought you were going to try to cozy up to Igor's gay son instead."

"That was the plan, but it changed."

"Why? Did something happen?"

I stared at her with my lips pressed together. I didn't want to lie to Aunt Maddy. But I didn't want to tell her the truth either.

Then she glanced down and spotted my white silk shirt in the wastebasket. Before I could stop her, she'd plucked it out. "What happened here?" she asked, poking her finger through the hole in the fabric.

"I tore it."

"I can see that. Care to explain how?"

I grabbed the shirt, balled it up, and tossed it back into the wastebasket. "It snagged on a file cabinet."

"How does someone snag the back of their shirt on a file cabinet?"

"It was an accident, okay? Accidents happen."

She folded her arms across her chest and stared at me. "I don't like this, Grace."

"I don't like it either, but we are where we are."

"No, we're here because you insisted. You don't have to do this. You can walk away."

I couldn't walk away, and she knew that. But we'd had this argument before and there was no point in having it again. Neither one of us was going to change the other's mind.

"Just promise you're being careful," she said.

"I promise."

Then she hugged me and I winced. She'd accidentally squeezed my bruise.

Of course, she demanded an explanation, and this time I couldn't get out of providing one. Then she wanted to see the bruise for herself. Then she lectured me again. This was my life now.

When she finally left my bedroom, I pulled my small suitcase down from the top of the closet and packed enough clothes for two days and nights in LA. I'd start looking for a rental house tomorrow, but until I found one, I'd stay in a hotel. I just couldn't face another five to six hours round trip in the car.

If I'd known at the time where I'd be sleeping the next night, and who I'd be sleeping with, I would've packed differently.

Chapter 15

When I arrived at the gallery the next morning, Igor and Sergey were waiting for me. I greeted Igor. Sergey, I ignored. Then I continued to my windowless office. Everything was exactly where I'd left it when I ran out the day before. My suit jacket was still hanging on the back of my chair, my briefcase was still sitting underneath the desk, and except for my phone and keys, the contents of my purse were still scattered across the top.

Igor followed me into the office and sat down on the couch. I didn't know where Sergey was, but I was happy not to have him in the room. "I'll go through these files today," I said, nodding at the stack of manila folders Sergey hadn't bothered to remove when I ran out yesterday. "Should I call you when I'm done?"

Before he could answer, the alarm beeped twice and I heard footsteps on the gallery floor. A minute later Alex appeared in the doorway.

"What are you doing here?" I asked.

Alex nodded at me, his usual greeting, then turned to Igor. "You wanted to see me?"

"Yes," Igor said. "You two are going to Oregon."

"Oregon?" I said. "Why the hell are we going to Oregon?" If Igor said he wanted us to go to Switzerland or the Cayman Islands, I would've been less surprised, since those two locations were well known hotspots for money laundering. But Oregon?

"There's a painting arriving tomorrow," Igor said to Alex. "It's being delivered to the storage facility in Coos Bay." Then Igor called out to Sergey, who appeared in the doorway with a black gym bag, which he handed to Alex. "You shouldn't have any trouble with Grace with you," Igor continued then stood up. "Call Sergey when it's done." Then he and Sergey walked out of the room.

I waited until I heard the alarm beep twice before I turned to Alex. "What the hell just happened?"

"Get your stuff together," he said, nodding to the mess on my desk. "We'll talk in the car. It's a long drive."

"Wait, we're *driving* to Oregon? Why can't we just fly there?"

Alex held up the gym bag. "Because you can't get on a commercial flight with half a million dollars."

WE DROVE to Alex's house first so he could pack a bag. Luckily, I'd already planned on spending the night in a hotel so all I had to do was transfer my suitcase from my car to Alex's trunk. If we'd had to stop in Santa Veneta first, it would've added an extra hour to our fourteen-hour trip.

"Did you remember to bring back my jacket?" Alex asked as he pulled into his driveway.

"Yes," I said. "It's in my suitcase. MJ recognized it, by the way."

"What did you tell him?" Alex asked as we both got out of his car.

"I told him I borrowed it from you."

Alex popped open his trunk and pulled out my suitcase. "And?"

"And nothing. I already told him I was doing some work for someone you knew in LA. Sofia wants to know when you're coming to visit by the way."

Alex carried my suitcase into his house. I unzipped it and pulled out his jacket.

"Thanks," he said as I handed it to him. "Wait here. I'll be right back."

I sat down on the living room couch and scanned the news on my phone while Alex disappeared into the back of the house. When he re-appeared five minutes later, his all-black outfit had been replaced with dark blue jeans, a gray half-zip sweater with a white T-shirt underneath, and running shoes. He had a duffel bag slung over one shoulder, and he was carrying the green jacket in one hand and his gun in the other.

"How do I look?" he asked.

"Good. It's nice to see you in a color other than black."

"I never wear black when I travel."

"Why not?"

He ignored my question and headed into the dining room. He opened the sideboard and pulled out a box that was large enough to hold a serving platter. He set it down on top of the cabinet, lifted the lid, placed the gun inside the box, and returned the box to the cabinet.

"You're not bringing your gun?" I asked.

"Can't," he said. "We're flying home."

Apparently, the prohibition on traveling in black applied to cars too. Instead of driving the BMW up the coast, Alex rented a burgundy sedan. Alex waited until we were headed north on I-5 before he explained how this worked.

"Igor's what you'd call a facilitator," he said. "He helps people buy and sell art."

"Isn't that what Mischa does?" I asked, adjusting my seat. The rental car was less flashy than Alex's BMW, but it was also a lot less comfortable. "Or is Igor the real owner of the gallery?" I hadn't seen Mischa since the exhibition last Saturday night. I had no idea what he did all day.

Alex shook his head. "This isn't for the gallery. The painting stays at the storage facility. We're only going up there to pay for it."

"I'm confused. Why is the painting staying in storage? And couldn't Igor have just wired the money?"

"Not if he doesn't want to have to answer questions about the source of the funds. Gallery sales are public. Mischa handles those when they happen. Igor handles the private sales."

Alex explained that in private art sales, both the buyer and seller can remain anonymous. Igor arranges for the sale to take place inside the storage facility because it resides in what's known as a Foreign Trade Zone or FTZ. According to Alex, there were hundreds of FTZs throughout the country, including some in California, but the Coos Bay FTZ had the advantage of being in Oregon, a state with no sales or use tax. Igor could import artwork from anywhere in the world duty free and sell it to anyone in the world too, and as long the artwork remained inside the FTZ storage facility, no taxes were due.

"Are FTZs the same as freeports?" I'd heard of those because Jonah and I had watched a story about them on one of the news shows. I only remembered because Jonah told me one of his wealthy clients had artwork stored in a freeport in Geneva. The client bought the painting for ten million dollars, then hired an artist to paint a counterfeit for fifty thousand, which he hung on the wall at his home in Carmel. But he kept the original in the freeport, where it remained in climate-controlled storage with twenty-four-hour security, increasing in value tax-free.

"I don't know," Alex said. "I've only been to the one in Coos Bay."

"And you do this for Igor a lot?"

"I used to. I haven't been in a while. Igor must think it's safe for me to go if I'm with you."

"Why would it be safer with me? Surely he knows you wouldn't steal from him."

Alex chuckled. "Nobody steals from Igor. Not if they want to live."

"Then why?"

Alex stared at me a moment then turned his attention back to the road. "Last time I made this trip I got pulled over. The cop said I was speeding. I probably was, but there were plenty of other cars going faster than me. I'm the one they pulled over."

"And you think it was intentional?"

"You don't?"

"I don't know. If lots of cars were speeding, they probably just picked someone at random."

Alex shook his head.

"Why don't you think so?" I asked.

He turned to me, angry now. "They used it as an excuse to search the car."

"The police can't search your car for a traffic stop, not without probable cause."

"Look at me, Grace. What do you see?"

I glanced over at Alex. "A man in his thirties?"

"A Hispanic man, alone, in an expensive car. That's probable cause."

"That is *not* probable cause."

"Well, this cop thought so. I'm lucky it happened on the

drive home. All I had with me was a bag of dirty clothes. That cop tore the car apart looking for drugs. He was not happy when he had to let me go with a speeding ticket. After that, Igor started sending one of the Russians. And now we always drive rental cars."

"Igor thinks rental cars are less likely to get stopped for speeding?"

"He thinks the cops will be a lot less suspicious of a man and woman on vacation, especially when the woman looks like you."

"Because I look so innocent?"

"Because you're white."

Chapter 16

ONCE WE WERE out of the city, the choice of radio stations got a lot worse, so I plugged in my headphones and opened my audiobook.

"You can play your music if you want," Alex said. "I like all kinds."

I pulled one earbud out of my ear. "It's not music, it's a novel."

"What's it about?"

I paused the narration and tapped the description. I'd bought it so long ago I couldn't remember anymore. "A British woman marries an American man and they move to his home in Kentucky where she starts delivering books by horseback as part of Eleanor Roosevelt's traveling library."

"Is it any good?"

"I don't know. I just started it. But the reviews are good."

"I'll give it a listen," he said.

"Really?" It didn't seem like the kind of story that would appeal to Alex.

"It's a long drive to Coos Bay."

We stopped once for gas, then again in a tiny town off the freeway that Alex insisted had a good restaurant. My hopes weren't high as we walked into the western-themed bar, but Alex was right. The food was delicious. When we got back into the car, I offered to drive but Alex insisted he was fine. He just asked me to turn up the volume on the book.

"I'm so surprised you like this," I said.

"Why? You think I never read a book before? I admit I've never listened to an audiobook before. You just download them to your phone like music?"

"Yup. One tap with your credit card."

"You mean gift card."

"I'm sure those work too, but isn't it easier just to use a credit card?"

"I don't have a credit card."

"How can you not have a credit card? Everyone has a credit card. How do you pay for things?"

"Cash. Like I did at the restaurant. Or gift cards if I want to buy online. You know the credit card companies track you, right?"

I'd never thought about it before, but it made sense. How else would they know to alert me about suspicious activity on my account. "I'm not sure I care if Visa knows I like Greek yogurt."

"That Visa card is issued by a bank. You see where I'm going with this?"

"Oh, right." I sometimes forgot what Alex did for a living. And I supposed what I did for a living now too. Although I wasn't involved in the drug side of the business, just the money laundering side, as if those two weren't intertwined. I tried not to dwell on my new vocation. I was doing this for Jonah and Amelia. I was working under the auspices of the FBI. I said I'd do whatever it took to take down Igor Volodnik. If that meant I had to work with criminals, even engage in what would otherwise be criminal behavior myself, then so be it.

We stopped for gas again after we crossed into Oregon and continued on I-5 for another hour. After we exited the freeway, we still drove another hour and half before we reached Coos Bay. Luckily, the book was long. It ended ten minutes before we arrived at the motel.

"Igor couldn't have sprung for a nicer place?" I said as Alex pulled into the parking lot of a weathered two-story building.

"This is the nicer place. Last time I stayed at the Motel 6 down the street."

I remained in the car with the bags while Alex went to the lobby to check in. He returned with the room key, which was an actual metal key attached to a plastic disc, and we drove another five hundred feet, where Alex parked in the space directly in front of our room. Alex carried our luggage, and I unlocked the door and flipped on the lights.

"You've got to be kidding me." The room wasn't as bad as I thought it would be from the outside. Management had obviously renovated sometime in the last thirty years. But the room only had one bed.

Alex came up behind me with the bags. "It's fine. I'll sleep on the floor."

"You can't sleep on the floor! I'll call the front desk. Maybe they have a rollaway. Or I'll get my own room."

Alex shut the door behind him and turned the lock on the deadbolt. "Igor booked this room because he thinks we're a couple. Everyone we come into contact with needs to think so too. No extra beds and no separate rooms. You can use the bathroom first if you want."

I washed my face, brushed my teeth, and changed into pajamas, which were really sleep shorts and a matching camisole top. If I'd known when I'd packed my bag last night that I'd be sharing a room with Alex, I would've brought something less revealing. I checked the closet for a complimentary bathrobe, but there wasn't one. It wasn't that kind of hotel. So I sprinted to the bed and burrowed in under the blanket.

When Alex went into the bathroom, I turned on the television. I was still flipping channels on the TV when he returned to the bedroom wearing only boxer-briefs. The tattoo, which I'd previously seen only the edges of snaking out from the top of his shirt or the bottom of his sleeve, was now revealed. It started at his neck and spread down one arm and partway across his chest. The light in the room was dim and he was standing far enough away that I couldn't make out the design. But I could clearly see his underwear.

"I thought you don't wear black when you travel," I said, trying not to stare. His body was lean and toned like Daniel's, but his hair was darker and Daniel was tattoo-free.

"What is this fascination you have with my clothes," he said as he grabbed a pillow off the bed and laid it on the floor with an extra blanket he must've pulled out of the closet.

"It's not a fascination," I said, clicking off the television. "More of a mild interest in your wardrobe."

"Maybe it's not my wardrobe you're interested in."

I could feel my cheeks heating up and I shut off the light. "Goodnight, Alex."

"Goodnight, Grace."

But it was obvious neither one of us was getting much sleep. I kept flipping from my back to my stomach to my side and to my back again, and I could hear Alex tossing and turning on the floor too. I wasn't surprised when I heard him get up and head into the bathroom. I was surprised when I heard the shower running.

When the bathroom door opened, I said, "Most people take a shower to wake up not to help them fall asleep."

"That's not why I took a shower."

"You just had a burning desire to feel clean at"—I glanced at the bedside clock—"one sixteen in the morning?"

"It was a cold shower."

"Oh." I couldn't deny I was having impure thoughts too. It had been many months since I'd last slept with Daniel and there hadn't been anyone else since. On a purely physical level, I was attracted to Alex. But I had no intention of acting on that desire. We worked together and would soon be living in the same house for half the week. It wasn't possible to have a one-night stand with him and I wasn't interested in anything else.

I put thoughts of Alex out of my head, but I still couldn't fall asleep. It was the unfamiliar surroundings and my anxiety about the next day. I really wished I still had my sleeping pills, but no doctor would prescribe them for me after my suicide attempt. So I practiced the deep breathing exercises I'd learned at the Wellstone Center until exhaustion finally overtook me.

I WOKE up the next morning when I heard Alex leave the room. It was early but I got out of bed to shower and dress. By the time Alex returned wearing gym shorts and a T-shirt drenched in sweat, I'd already repacked my suitcase. "I'll give you some privacy," I said and stepped outside. The morning air was cool and, although the pavement was dry, the sky was a solid white-gray. It looked like it might rain at any moment.

I followed the cement walkway to the lobby and discovered the motel had a restaurant. I ate breakfast alone and, by the time I returned to the room, Alex was waiting for me. He'd showered and was wearing the same jeans as yesterday, but today's sweater was navy blue and he wore his green utility jacket over it.

"I brought you coffee," I said and handed him the to-go cup.

"Thanks," he said. "We should go."

"Where to?" I asked.

"To see a painting. Today you're an art dealer."

Chapter 17

ALEX DROVE us to a large industrial office park only a few miles away from the motel. I was wearing a black pantsuit and high heels because, when I'd packed my bag, I'd thought I'd be going to the office today. I looked the part of an art dealer, or what I imagined an art dealer might look like, but I was concerned Alex and I were mismatched since he was dressed more casually. He didn't think it was a problem.

"No one will see me," he said. "You're going in alone."

My heart started pounding in my chest. "Alone? Why are you sending me in alone?" I'd assumed Alex would be there to protect me, although from what I wasn't sure.

He pulled into a parking space in front of a nondescript warehouse. "You'll be fine. You don't have to do anything."

"If I don't have to do anything, then why do I have to go?"

He fished a piece of paper out of his jacket pocket and handed it to me. It contained a long, handwritten number. "Go inside and tell the manager you're there to authenticate this shipment."

"How do I authenticate it? I don't know anything about it."

"You don't have to," he said. "Just confirm the painting's there. Javier knows better than to screw Igor over with a fake."

"What about the money? Don't I need to pay?"

"No, I'll be handling that part."

I exited the car and walked to the door of the warehouse. But when I pulled on the handle, it was locked. Then I noticed the buzzer. I pushed the red button and smiled up at the security camera.

It was a man's voice on the intercom. "May I help you?"

"I'm here to authenticate a painting."

"Item number?" he asked.

I read off the number Alex had written down and a few seconds later the door unlocked. I walked into a tiny vestibule. The man from the intercom was seated behind a desk with a computer and there were three molded plastic chairs lined up against the outer wall. On the opposite wall was a heavy metal door protecting whatever was inside.

"Have a seat," the man said. He looked to be about my age and was dressed in khakis and a polo shirt, but he had no badge or key card and there was no insignia on his clothing to indicate where he worked.

I sat down on one of the hard plastic chairs and waited. A few minutes later the inner metal door opened and another man appeared. This man was older and obviously higher up the corporate food chain. His hair was gray and thinning and he wore an expensive dark blue suit with a lavender shirt and tie. He didn't tell me his name or ask me for mine. He just said, "Welcome. Please come inside." Then he held the door open for me.

I walked into a giant warehouse filled with rows and rows of movable metal shelves. It reminded me of my college library, until the man in the suit separated two of the shelves to create an aisle for us to walk down. Instead of books, the metal shelves were filled with paintings.

The man stopped midway down the aisle and subtly pointed to a landscape oil painting in an ornate gold frame. I had no idea who had painted it and I was too embarrassed to ask. I stared at the image of the lake surrounded by birds and marshy grass for a few seconds then turned to the man and smiled. "Thank you."

He nodded and motioned for me to walk back the way we came. He accompanied me back through the warehouse and into the reception area. I had my hand on the knob of the outer door when he stopped me. "Miss, you still need to sign."

I turned back and found the gentleman holding a clipboard. It contained a single sheet of paper, which I briefly scanned. It stated the name of the artist and the painting, neither of which were familiar to me, the item number, and an acknowledgment that the shipment wasn't damaged.

"I, um—"

He reached inside his suit jacket and pulled out a pen, an expensive one.

I took the heavy silver pen, scribbled something illegible on the signature line, and handed the pen and the clipboard back to him.

He glanced down at my signature. "Very good." He smiled.

I smiled back at him and the younger man still seated at the desk, then left the building.

When I slid into the passenger seat of the rental car, Alex asked, "How did it go?"

I let out the breath I didn't realize I'd been holding and felt my shoulders drop. "Fine. I think. Although if I had to explain what happened in there, I don't think I could."

"That's the point," Alex said and started the engine. He drove back onto the main road and the local airport quickly came into view. It consisted of just one squat building and a hangar surrounded by a dozen private planes. Alex drove through the entrance, but instead of turning into the parking lot, he continued onto the tarmac.

"Where are you going?" I asked, but he didn't answer.

Alex pulled up next to a small jet with its staircase down. "Wait here," he said before he hopped out of the car. He grabbed the gym bag out of the trunk, and walked it up the steps of the private plane. He reappeared a minute later, minus the gym bag, and slid in behind the wheel of the rental car.

"What just happened?" I asked.

"We've got a couple of hours before our flight," he said. "Is there anything you'd like to see before we leave?"

Chapter 18

ALEX KNEW of a nearby state park so we drove there. But as soon as we arrived, it started to rain. We abandoned our sightseeing plans and drove to the shopping mall we'd passed on the highway. It was old and rundown and half the storefronts were empty, but it was warm and dry and we had an hour to kill. I dragged Alex toward the mall's only clothing store, a Ross Dress For Less.

He stopped at the entrance with his hands in his pockets. "I hate shopping."

"So did my husband. That didn't mean he didn't have to come. C'mon, fake boyfriend. You need a wardrobe redo."

Alex rolled his eyes, but he followed me inside.

I took him to outerwear first. "Sorry to be the one to tell you this, but green is not your color." I handed him a gray fleece and a blue shirt-jacket and we moved onto pants. I held up a pair of khakis. "Nothing says I'm an innocent suburban dad and definitely not a drug dealer more than these."

"No," Alex said.

"You don't have to get the tan," I said and returned the khakis to the rack. "They have other colors. How about gray?"

Alex nodded reluctantly.

I pulled two more pairs of pants off the rack and a few pairs of designer jeans and sent him into the dressing room. He eventually emerged wearing his own clothes and holding the gray pants and the blue shirt-jacket.

"That's it?" I asked.

"Yes. Are we done?"

"Almost." I led him into the leather goods section. "You need a wallet."

"Why do I need a wallet?"

"Because only drug dealers walk around carrying a wad of cash wrapped in a rubber band."

I handed Alex a black leather billfold and he attempted to stuff it into the front pocket of his jeans.

"Back pocket," I said.

"That's just asking to be pickpocketed."

"Every man I know keeps their wallet in their back pocket."

Alex rolled his eyes but stuck the wallet into his back pocket. "This isn't even comfortable."

I lifted my leg and pointed to my high-heeled shoe. "You think these are comfortable? Suck it up, buttercup."

Alex added the wallet to his pile. "Are we done now?" he whined.

"Yes. And the best part is we're in Oregon, so I just saved you nine and a half percent sales tax."

Even with the shopping excursion and dropping off the rental car we still made it back to the airport with plenty of time to spare. The security line at the Coos Bay Airport was much shorter than any security line I'd ever waited in at LAX. We flew from Coos Bay to San Francisco on a small commuter jet, then changed to a much larger plane for our connecting flight to

LA. By the time I finally made it back to Santa Veneta that evening, MJ's basketball game was half over. But he seemed happy to see me anyway. I'd promised him I'd be there if I could.

"You're leaving again?" Aunt Maddy said when she came down to the kitchen the next morning and found me dressed in a suit.

"Just for the day," I said. "I'll be home for dinner."

At least that was the plan. But Agent Diaz called and said he needed to debrief me and Alex and the only time he could meet with us was that night. This time we rendezvoused in the parking lot of a big box hardware store.

"What do you think?" I asked Agent Diaz after I'd told him everything I could remember. "Can you build a case?"

"On what?" Agent Diaz said. "You went to a warehouse and looked at a painting. That's not a crime."

"What about the money?" I said. "Alex paid in cash."

Agent Diaz shook his head. "Settle in, Grace. This may take a while."

I sighed and closed my eyes. It was only the first week and I was already exhausted.

"Rent a house here," Agent Diaz said. "At least you won't have the commute. That'll make it easier."

I nodded. "How long of a lease should I get?"

"At least six months."

"Six months!"

Agent Diaz turned to Alex. "Go with her to look since you'll be staying there too."

Chapter 19

"This is so much harder than I thought it would be," I said to Dr. Rubenstein during our weekly appointment. I'd been spending Tuesdays through Thursdays in LA for the last several months, so I met with Dr. Rubenstein on Friday mornings when I was in Santa Veneta.

"In what way?" she asked.

"When I proposed this plan to Agent Diaz, I was so focused on seeing Igor behind bars I didn't really think through what it would be like to have to work for him. I can't look at him without thinking *but for you, Jonah and Amelia would be alive.* Do you know what that's like?"

"Hard, I'm sure."

"Some days it takes all of my willpower not to just reach across the desk and strangle him."

Dr. Rubenstein nodded sympathetically.

"Not that I could even if I tried. He probably weighs double what I do, and Sergey is always lurking nearby. And if that's not bad enough, I feel like a giant fraud too."

"A fraud?"

"I spend half the week in LA pretending to be someone I'm

not, and then I come home and lie to my family about what I'm doing when I'm not with them. I hate lying all the time. I feel awful. And the most frustrating part is I don't even know if it's going to work. It's been three months already, and I still have nothing."

"Three months isn't very long for an investigation."

"I know. Agent Diaz tells me that all the time. He says I need to be patient; that investigations take time."

"That's true," Dr. Rubenstein said. Her daughter-in-law worked for the DEA so she was familiar with the practical aspects of undercover investigations and the toll they can take on an agent's family.

"I know I'm the one who wanted this, but I don't know how much longer I can keep it up. The lines are already starting to blur."

"How so?"

I shifted in my seat. I wasn't sure exactly how much I was allowed to tell Dr. Rubenstein. Agent Diaz's blanket admonition that the investigation was confidential and I couldn't talk about it with anyone was ringing in my ears. But I had never stuck to that completely. My aunt knew some things because I'd told her I asked Agent Diaz to make me a confidential informant before he'd agreed. Plus, on a practical level, I had to tell her why I was suddenly living in LA for half the week.

Dr. Rubenstein also knew some of it because it was her daughter-in-law who had unwittingly revealed that my brother-in-law Jake was a current FBI agent and not a former one. When I'd confronted him, he finally broke down and told me the truth about why Jonah was killed and his own involvement too. As with my aunt, Dr. Rubenstein already knew about some of my activities because I'd discussed it with her before Agent Diaz had agreed to make me a confidential informant. But I still wasn't sure how much I should tell her now.

"Everything I say in here is confidential, right? You can't disclose it to anyone."

"Almost everything," she said. "If you told me you actually planned to kill Igor, I'd have to alert the police. But if you disclose information about your undercover work for the FBI, that's confidential."

I nodded and took a deep breath. This was weighing on me so heavily I really wanted to talk to someone about it. "A surprising amount of what I do for Igor is actually normal legal work. I mean, the invoices and payments are questionable because I know those companies exist only on paper, but even that's not necessarily illegal. But preparing contracts, reviewing documents, moving assets around, I did all that for legitimate clients when I worked for the firm here in Santa Veneta before I went out on maternity leave.

"And I actually like Mischa. He doesn't come into the office that often, but when he does, we always have a good time. He takes me with him sometimes to look at art he's considering for the gallery. Then we usually go out afterwards to eat, or shop, or both. He has a great eye for fashion and he's funny too. I mean, if his father wasn't responsible for my family's murder, and I wasn't trying to put them all in prison, he and I could actually be friends."

Dr. Rubenstein nodded. "It's not uncommon to have warm feelings toward the people you're investigating. Even agents who are trained to do this kind of work have a hard time with it."

"I have no warm feelings for Igor. And Sergey's a pig. But I feel like if Mischa had been born into a different family, he wouldn't be a criminal. He's actually a decent human being. I feel bad that he's going to get caught up in all this."

"Will he?" she asked. "Couldn't he testify against his father too?"

I shook my head. "He wouldn't. He's too afraid of him. Rightfully so."

Dr. Rubenstein nodded again.

After a short silence I said, "And it's not just the job I'm having a hard time with."

"No?"

"It's Alex too."

Chapter 20

Dr. Rubenstein sat in silence while I tried to figure out how best to explain what had been gnawing at me for months.

"I don't work with Alex. Not directly. He does whatever he does during the day, and I don't ask questions and Alex doesn't offer any information. I don't want to know about the drug business and he knows that. The work I do for Igor just involves money laundering."

Dr. Rubenstein took a deep breath and waited for me to continue.

"We really only see each other in the evenings when we're both at the house. But I have to eat and he has to eat, so we eat together. Sometimes he cooks dinner for the two of us and sometimes I do and sometimes neither one of us feels like cooking and we order in. Afterwards, unless he has a late-night meeting, which happens occasionally but not often, we'll watch TV together or a movie until we go to bed. *Separate* beds," I added in case she had any doubt.

"But even though we sleep in separate bedrooms, it still almost feels like we're a couple. I mean, when Jonah was alive, we did pretty much the same thing in the evenings, except we slept in the same bed."

Dr. Rubenstein hesitated then said, "I think it's understandable you would feel that way. You are cohabitating."

"Except we're not a couple. It's all pretend."

"Is it?"

"I just told you we sleep in separate bedrooms. In case it's not clear, he and I have never had sex. We've never even kissed."

"Do you want to have sex with Alex?"

And there it was. Ever since our trip to Oregon, this was the thought that kept me up at night and gnawed at me during the day. Alex was the exact opposite of Jonah in almost every way, yet I couldn't deny my attraction to him. And this disturbed me. I didn't know what to do with these feelings.

"How can you even ask me that? He's a drug dealer. Even if he is a confidential informant for the FBI, he's still a drug dealer. I can't condone that. Plus, once he testifies against Igor, he goes into Witness Protection. So even if I did want a relationship with him, which I don't because, did I mention he's a drug dealer, there is absolutely no future with Alex. None. It's not even a remote possibility."

"Why does there have to be a future?" she asked. "Can't you just enjoy his company for the time you're together?"

"What would be the point of that?"

Dr. Rubenstein laughed. "I don't know, Grace. Maybe sleeping with Alex would be a pleasurable experience and make you happy."

That's when I suddenly teared up.

"What just happened?" she asked. "Are you thinking about Jonah?"

I shrugged and pulled a tissue from the box next to the couch. "I'm always thinking about Jonah. Why should this day be any different?"

"It's been two years, Grace. You're entitled to find happiness with someone else."

"Even a drug dealer?"

"The heart wants what the heart wants."

"I don't think it's my heart that wants him."

Dr. Rubenstein chuckled. "Well, whatever body part it is, you're drawn to him. I agree this is unlikely to lead to a long-term relationship, but you're both consenting adults. If you want to enjoy each other's company in the meantime, you should. There's nothing inherently wrong with that."

Then why did it feel wrong?

Chapter 21

Alex's birthday was the following week. I only knew because MJ told me. I insisted we celebrate and, since Alex's birthday fell on a Wednesday and we'd both be working in LA that day, we agreed we would celebrate in Santa Veneta with the kids the following weekend.

I made a dinner reservation at a family-friendly restaurant and Sofia decided that she and my aunt would bake a cake—chocolate with chocolate frosting because that was Sofia's favorite. I didn't know if chocolate was Alex's favorite flavor too, but I was sure he'd eat a slice anyway.

We invited Maria to join us, but she declined because she had to work that night. She'd gotten a waitressing job at a restaurant on the pier. We all knew once she had saved up enough money for her own apartment, she was going to petition the court to regain custody of the kids. But we didn't talk about that. Talking about it made it real.

I offered to take Alex out to dinner on his actual birthday too, but he declined, so I bought steaks at the grocery store and cooked dinner at home. The house we'd rented was fully furnished and had a built-in barbecue, as well as a pool, four bedrooms, five bathrooms, and a beautiful city-lights view. It was the first house Alex and I looked at together and although we both liked it, I thought we should try to find someplace less expensive. I made appointments for us to look at two more houses the next day when Alex called and told me he'd rented the first house and had paid the six-month lease in advance. I'd asked him if he was paying for it or whether the FBI was covering the expense. I never did get a straight answer.

Since the house had four bedrooms, I'd been thinking about bringing the kids down to LA for the summer to give my aunt a break. She hadn't complained about taking care of the kids on her own for half the week, but I still felt guilty. Fostering them had been my idea, and I'd promised her we would do it together. Now I just had to get Alex to agree.

I wasn't sure how he was going to react. I knew Alex loved the kids, but both he and MJ had told me after Alex and Maria's mother died, they all lived together for a short time and it hadn't gone well. I didn't know whether it was because of friction with Maria, friction with the kids, or just too many people in too small a space.

Bringing the kids to LA for the summer was also complicated because Maria had court-ordered visitation rights. Someone—and I intended to nominate Alex for this job—needed to talk to Maria and get her to agree. Therefore, my cooking dinner for Alex had a dual purpose. I wanted to do something nice for him on his birthday, but I was also trying to butter him up.

Since it was a warm night, I suggested we eat dinner on the patio so we could enjoy the view. Alex agreed and together we carried the food outside. I went back to the kitchen to fetch our drinks and returned with a glass of red wine for me and a bottle of beer for Alex.

"How come I don't get wine?" he asked.

"You can have wine if you want," I said. "I thought you preferred beer."

He shrugged. "I feel like mixing it up tonight."

I swapped his beer for a wine glass, and this time I brought the bottle of Cabernet Sauvignon with me. In my absence, Alex lit two small candles and placed them in the center of the patio table. I poured him a glass of wine and sat down.

"Bon appétit," I said, and we clinked glasses.

We dug into our steaks, grilled asparagus, and baked potatoes, and as was our custom, we didn't talk about work, his or mine. I waited until he was on his second glass of wine before I brought up my idea.

"I was thinking," I said, swishing the wine in my glass, "maybe we should bring the kids to LA for the summer."

Alex didn't look up from his plate. "I thought you wanted to keep them far away from Igor."

"I do, but it's not like we socialize with him. They'll never see him. They'll just be here with us. My aunt's been on her own with them for half the week for months. I'd like to give her a break."

Alex shrugged. "It's okay with me."

Huh. That was easier than I'd expected. "Great. I'll start looking into camps."

"Camps?"

"Yes. Sofia needs to go to camp."

"Why does she need to go to camp? I don't know anyone who's gone to camp."

I didn't mention I went to day camp every summer from the time I was a kindergartener until I was a teenager, at which point my parents sent me to sleepaway camp. "I'll be working and so will you. Are you suggesting we leave her alone in the house all day?"

"MJ can watch her."

"MJ's sixteen. The last thing he wants to do is spend the summer babysitting his little sister."

"Then what's he going to do?"

"Well, I was hoping he'd get a job."

Alex swallowed a big gulp of wine and smacked his lips. "I'm in favor of that, but where? I assume you don't want him working for me."

"You assume correct. I was thinking maybe he could find a job as a camp counselor. Or if he doesn't want to do that, then he can work retail or mow loans or valet. Honestly, I don't care what he does as long as it keeps him busy and out of trouble."

"Okay by me," Alex said.

"The only problem is Maria," I continued. "She has visitation rights, and I'm sure she's not going to waive them. But I was thinking I could drive the kids back to Santa Veneta on weekends and she can see them then."

Alex nodded. "Seems reasonable."

"To us. But the plan only works if Maria agrees."

"She'll agree," he said. "It won't be a problem."

I took that to mean he would convince her. "Great. Once we know what the kids are doing for the summer, we can work out a schedule for you and me."

"Why do we need a schedule?"

I thought it was obvious. "Someone has to drive them back and forth to camp and work every day. You weren't thinking that was going to be all my job, did you?"

"It's not?" Alex said.

I laughed. I couldn't tell if he was teasing me or if he genuinely believed taking care of the kids was solely my responsibility. "Nice try, Alex. Welcome to the twenty-first century. Men care for children too. They've been enlightened by the women in their lives." Just like I'm going to enlighten you.

Chapter 22

After we finished eating, Alex offered to help me clear the table.

"See," I said, "I've already enlightened you. I bet you never used to help clear the table before you met me."

We both laughed.

"Thank you for offering," I continued, "but no one has to clean on their birthday."

"Is that a law?" he asked.

"Yes, Grace's law. Look it up."

He laughed again and sat back down and I carried our dirty dishes into the kitchen and stacked them in the sink with the rest of the soiled pans. I returned to the patio with a red velvet cupcake with a lit candle in the center of it.

"I thought we were celebrating over the weekend," he said.

"We are. But someone has to sing *Happy Birthday* to you on your actual birthday too."

"Another law?"

"Yes. And you're also required to make a wish and blow out the candle."

Alex smiled as I sang an off-tune version of *Happy*

Birthday, then he blew out the candle and split the cupcake in two. After we'd each eaten half, I returned to the house to fetch his gift.

"Presents too?" he said when I handed him a small, square box, which had been expertly wrapped by the store's saleswoman. I'd purchased the gift on my lunch hour. It didn't take long because I knew exactly what I was looking for.

"It's something small," I said. "No big deal."

Alex ripped off the silver paper and lifted the lid. When he reached inside and pulled out the two-inch strip of black leather, he looked confused.

"It's a money clip. In case your rubber band ever breaks." I'd never seen him use the wallet I insisted he buy when we were in Oregon.

Alex stood up and pulled his wad of cash out of his front pocket. He replaced the rubber band with the money clip and shoved the bills back into his jeans. Then he sat down again. "I like it. It's comfortable."

"Good," I said and held up my wine glass. "To money clips."

"And pretend girlfriends," he replied and clinked his glass against mine. He poured what little wine was left in the bottle into both our glasses. "Movie tonight?"

"Sure." It was our usual routine. "I just need to do the dishes first."

"The dishes can wait."

This was part of our usual routine too. I liked to clean up the kitchen as soon as we finished eating, but Alex preferred to leave the dirty dishes in the sink until right before he went to bed, sometimes even waiting until the next morning to load them into the dishwasher. "You know I hate leaving a mess."

"It's my birthday. That means you have to do what I want, right?"

"Within reason," I said skeptically.

"Leaving dirty dishes in the sink for a couple hours while we watch a movie is reasonable. Even you have to agree."

I did. So when he opened the patio door and motioned me inside, I ignored the mess in the kitchen and headed into the living room. Alex turned on the television and clicked over to one of the streaming channels. A teaser for *Out of Africa* popped up on the screen.

"Looks interesting," he said. "What do you think?"

"I love that movie. I think it won an Academy Award for best picture."

"Huh. I've never seen it. Would you mind watching it again?"

"Not at all."

That was my first big mistake of the evening. But not my last.

Chapter 23

We sat next to each other on the couch, each with our shoes off and our feet up on the coffee table, while we sipped what was left of our wine and watched Robert Redford and Meryl Streep fall in love. I made it as far as the safari scene where Robert Redford washes Meryl Streep's hair before I started bawling.

Alex didn't ask me why I was crying. He was smart enough to figure that out on his own. He just put his arm around my shoulder and left it there while I cried. Eventually, the moment passed, as they always did, and I wiped my eyes. "Sorry about that," I said, and reached for a tissue to blow my nose.

"It's okay," Alex replied.

"You can turn it back on." Alex had paused the movie when I started crying. I would've un-paused it myself, but the remote was sitting next to him on the other side of the couch.

"We can watch something else if you want."

"No, let's finish," I said and a few more tears trickled out. "You have to see how it ends."

But instead of un-pausing the movie, Alex left the remote

where it was and turned to me. He placed both his hands on my face and wiped away my tears with his thumbs.

I froze. I knew what was going to happen next.

Bad idea, Grace. Really, really bad idea.

But it feels so good. Doesn't that matter?

Eating a hot fudge sundae for dinner feels good too. But then you feel sick afterwards. This is a mistake.

Dr. Rubenstein wouldn't say it's a mistake. She'd say it's perfectly fine for two consenting adults to watch a romantic movie together and then for one of said consenting adults to break down in tears because she missed her dead husband and the other consenting adult to wipe away her tears and kiss her, which Alex hadn't done yet, but I knew he was going to.

Then you and Dr. Rubenstein can agree to disagree because you KNOW this is a bad idea.

I did know. But when Alex leaned in and kissed me, I kissed him back.

And that's not all I did.

Chapter 24

ALEX DIDN'T KISS like Jonah or Daniel, or even Jake, although my memory of that night with Jake when I attempted suicide was a little fuzzy. Alex's kiss was insistent, demanding. He wanted all of me and he wanted me now. And I wanted him too.

He pulled my shirt over my head, and I let him.

Then he laid down on top of me and I could feel his erection through his jeans. But I didn't pull away. Instead, I hooked my leg over his, pulling him closer.

I was still wearing my bra, but the material was thin. Alex teased my breast through the gauzy fabric, and I let him. Then he pushed the fabric aside and sucked on my nipple, and I let him do that too.

His style was rougher than I was used to. There was no finesse, just naked desire. But it didn't deter me. If anything, it made me want him more.

Then my cell phone, which was sitting on the coffee table, buzzed. We both ignored it as Alex unzipped his jeans. It buzzed again while I wriggled out of my pants. And it kept buzzing until eventually I could no longer ignore it.

"I'm sorry," I said, pushing Alex off me. We were both still wearing our underwear, but I doubted we would be for long. "I have to answer this." Then I sat upright and reached for my phone. It was MJ's name on the caller ID.

"Hey, MJ, what's up?" I said, trying to sound normal and not all like someone who was about to have sex with his uncle.

"It's Aunt Maddy." He sounded out of breath, as if he'd just come home from a run. "Something's wrong."

I jumped up from the couch. "What's wrong? Is she okay?"

"I don't know," he said. "I can't understand what she's saying and she's kind of walking funny."

I started pacing the living room. "Is she drunk?"

"I didn't see her drink nothing with dinner," he said. "Just water."

"Put her on the phone. Let me talk to her." I noticed Alex pulled his jeans back up and I reached for my pants too.

I recognized my aunt's voice, but her words were slurred and I couldn't understand what she was saying. I yelled MJ's name until he took the phone back.

"See what I mean," he said.

"Get the landline and call nine-one-one right now."

"But—"

"Just do it!" I screamed.

I heard the 911 operator ask him what was his emergency.

"Tell her you're home with your aunt and she's having some kind of medical issue. Tell them they need to send an ambulance."

I coached him through the rest of the 911 operator's questions then told him I'd call him back and hung up. I needed to call my mother.

"What can I do?" Alex, now fully clothed, asked.

He'd heard everything so I didn't need to explain. "Nothing," I said as I tapped on my mother's number.

Alex handed me my shirt, which I pulled over my head

while I listened to the phone ring, willing my mother to pick up. When she didn't, I left her a voicemail telling her it was urgent and to call me back right away. Then I turned to Alex. "I have to go home. Let Igor know I won't be in tomorrow. Tell him I had a family emergency."

"Sure," he said.

I ran to my bedroom for my shoes and purse. When I came back into the hallway, Alex was waiting for me with his keys in his hand. "I'll drive."

"You don't need—"

"You're not going alone, Grace. I'm coming with you."

I WAS glad Alex had insisted on driving. It left me free to bounce back and forth between calls with my mother and MJ. When the ambulance arrived at my aunt's house, I insisted MJ stay home with Sofia. I told him I would go directly to the hospital, and I'd call him as soon as I knew anything.

When Alex and I arrived at the emergency room, the doctor informed us my aunt had suffered a stroke but she was in stable condition.

"She received treatment quickly," the doctor said. "That's the good news. We have no reason to think she won't make a full recovery, but it'll take time. Is there anyone at home who can care for her?"

"Yes," I said. My mom and I would figure something out.

"Good," the doctor said. "They're admitting her now. Once she's in a room, you can go up and see her."

I thanked the doctor and collapsed onto the hard plastic chair in the waiting room. Alex sat with me until the nurse allowed me to go upstairs to my aunt's room. Alex offered to accompany me, but I declined. "Will you stay at my aunt's house tonight? I don't like leaving MJ and Sofia there by themselves and someone needs to make sure they get to school in the morning."

"Sure," he said. "Whatever you need."

"Thanks," I replied and headed to the elevators.

When I walked into my aunt's hospital room I was taken aback. Obviously, I knew she'd had a stroke, but the reality of it didn't hit me until I saw her. In my mind, she was the aunt of my youth who I used to ride bikes with and who would stay up late with me and let me watch R-rated movies. The person in the hospital bed hooked up to beeping monitors was an old woman I didn't recognize. I announced my presence and squeezed her hand, but my aunt didn't move. The nurse told me she was sedated, but I could stay if I wanted. I spent the night fitfully dozing in the chair next to her bed.

In the morning I called Alex and asked if he would be willing to pick up my mother from the airport. She was flying in from San Francisco on an early flight. He agreed and brought her directly to the hospital.

I wasn't sure how much my aunt had told my mother about Alex, but since my mother was preoccupied with my aunt's medical condition, she didn't ask me any questions about him. That day would come though. I was sure of it.

THE DOCTORS KEPT my aunt in the hospital for five days. They could've discharged her to a rehabilitation center since it was covered by her insurance, but she didn't want to go. She wanted to come home. Since she couldn't manage the stairs yet, we converted the dining room into a bedroom for her and used the living room for her at-home therapy. My mother slept in my aunt's bedroom, and if Alex spent the night in Santa Veneta, which he did a few times, he stayed at my house in the Hills.

Igor had been understanding at first and had even sent

flowers to my aunt's hospital room. But by week two he wanted to know when I'd be back in LA. He still insisted we conduct all business in-person.

"I don't know what I'm going to do," I cried. It was just me and my mother at the kitchen table. My aunt and the kids were all asleep.

"Go back to work," she said. "I'll take care of Maddy."

As far as my mother knew, Igor was a legitimate client and, at the moment, the only one I had. "What about the kids?" I said. They still had two more weeks of school.

"Sofia's very sweet," my mom said, "but I'm not sure I can take care of her and Maddy at the same time. Does MJ have his driver's license yet? Maybe he could help."

I shook my head. My dad had taught me to drive when I was sixteen, but we hadn't even gotten MJ his learner's permit yet. "Before all this happened, Alex and I were talking about bringing the kids down to LA for the summer." Although I'd been so preoccupied with my aunt's recovery I hadn't actually made any plans.

"I think that's a good idea. They'll be bored at home with us all summer."

"Alex still needs to clear it with Maria first. He's driving up tomorrow. I'll talk to him about it then."

My mom reached for her mug and stood up. "You want coffee?" she asked, walking towards my aunt's old drip coffeemaker. "It's decaf."

"There is no point in drinking decaffeinated coffee." We'd had this friendly argument before.

"We'll see if you still feel that way when you're my age." My mother refilled her mug and joined me at the table again. We sat together in silence, the only sound in the room the ticking of the kitschy wall clock, until my mom said, "Do you ever plan on telling me what's going on with you and Alex?"

I kept my eyes focused on my water glass. "There's nothing to tell. He's MJ and Sofia's uncle. You know that."

"And you spend half the week living together in LA, but you sleep in separate bedrooms."

She had obviously discussed this with my aunt. "Yes."

"Yes? That's it? No explanation?"

I sighed. "It's not that I don't want to explain." That was a lie. The last thing I wanted to do was tell my mother that my new client was actually a Russian crime boss responsible for the murder of her son-in-law and granddaughter, but I was only working for him because I was a confidential informant for the FBI. "It's just better if you don't know." That was true.

"Better for who?"

"All of you. Aunt Maddy and the kids don't know either, and Alex and I want to keep it that way."

"Alex and I want to keep it that way?" she parroted back.

I didn't respond.

"Honestly, Grace, do you really expect me to believe you two are just roommates who sleep in separate bedrooms?"

"We do sleep in separate bedrooms!"

"I'm not blind, Grace. I see the way he looks at you."

"How does he look at me?"

"Well, not like someone who's sleeping in a separate bedroom!"

I thought back to the night of his birthday, which felt like months ago instead of only ten days, and sighed. "I swear to you, Mom, Alex and I have never slept together. The only reason we're living together is because I didn't want to have to commute from Santa Veneta to LA. That's why I spend half the week there and half the week here." Surely Aunt Maddy had told her that too.

"And you couldn't just rent your own apartment in LA? You have to stay with Alex?"

I sighed. "It's complicated. We're working on a project together. But I can't tell you about it, so don't ask."

"Right," my mother said. "The secret project."

I wondered again how much my aunt had told her. "Yes, Mom, it's confidential. But you'll be happy to know, I actually do have a plan."

My mother huffed. "And since when does anything ever go according to plan."

Chapter 25

Alex drove up to Santa Veneta Friday afternoon. We took the kids out to dinner and brought back take-out for my mom and my aunt, but by the time we arrived home, my aunt had already fallen asleep. I was concerned that my aunt seemed to be sleeping a lot, but her doctor said it was a good sign. Something about sleep being beneficial for the brain's neuroplasticity.

I didn't want my mom to eat dinner alone, so I asked Alex to help Sofia with her bath. "She can wash by herself," I said. "She just needs help with her hair."

"Sure," he said.

But my mother said, "No, Grace, you go. I'd like to talk to Alex."

"About what?" I asked.

"Nothing in particular," she replied.

I didn't believe that for a second. She was going to pump him for information.

Alex placed his hand on my shoulder and left it there. The gesture did not go unnoticed by my mother. "It's okay," he said. "I'll stay with your mom while you help Sofia."

"I don't need help," Sofia said to Alex, "but I want you to read me a story."

"That's fine, sweetheart," my mother said to Sofia. "When you're ready for a story, I'll send your uncle upstairs."

That mollified her. I kept Sofia company while she bathed, then helped her rinse the shampoo from her hair. I'd just helped her into her pajamas when Alex appeared in her doorway. I left the two of them alone, checked on MJ, who was chatting online with his friends, then went back downstairs to the kitchen where my mother was loading her dirty plate and silverware into the dishwasher.

"Did he answer all your questions?" I asked.

She shut the dishwasher and turned around. "No. He's even more tight-lipped than you."

"I could've told you that."

"Just promise me whatever you two are up to, you're staying safe."

"We are, Mom. I promise." I recalled Agent Diaz's description of Alex's job—to keep me alive—but I didn't share that with my mother. I didn't think it would help her sleep at night.

I needed to go back to my own house to pick up more clothes. Alex offered to drive me since my car was still down in LA. My mother and I had been sharing my aunt's old Subaru for the past ten days.

"I assume my mother grilled you about us," I said as Alex pulled out onto the street.

"Yup."

"Sorry about that. She's like a dog with a bone."

He reached over the gear shift and squeezed my hand. "Runs in the family, I guess."

That was the most noticeable change between us since the night of his birthday. Alex hadn't made any more sexual overtures, but he would casually touch me now and he never used to before.

"You need to talk to Maria and get her to sign off on the new visitation schedule," I said, casually pulling my hand away from his. "I'll look into camps for Sofia and a job for MJ."

"Okay. If she asks why, what do you want me to tell her?"

I sighed. I didn't want to give Maria any ammunition to use against us in the custody case. But I didn't want to ask the kids to lie for us either. And Sofia was so young she'd probably let it slip anyway. "Tell her we thought it would be better for the kids if they spent the summer with us in LA. I'll still bring them back to see her once a week anyway, so it shouldn't really matter to her where they are the rest of the time as long as they're safe."

"And their social worker?" he asked. "Is she going to be okay with them spending the summer with me?"

"I'll ask Janelle to talk to her. They have a good relationship. And she should know by now they're safe with me even if I'm not their legal guardian."

Alex parked in my driveway and we both got out. I was still fishing my keys out of my purse when he unlocked the front door with the spare key I'd given him after my aunt's stroke. He'd slept at my house several times in the last couple weeks.

When I went upstairs to my bedroom, Alex followed me. He sat on my bed while I tossed shorts and T-shirts into a shopping bag along with my sandals and some extra underwear. It was almost summer, and the weather had already turned warm.

I quickly finished and shut off the closet light. "I'm done. Let's go."

Alex patted the space next to him on the bed.

"No," I said.

"I just want to talk."

"We can talk in the car."

Alex leaned back on his elbows and stared at me.

"Oh, fine." I dropped my shopping bag on the floor and laid down next to him on the bed. "What's on your mind?"

He reached over and placed his warm hand on my abdomen. "You," he said.

As soon as his skin touched mine I felt tingly all over, but I pushed his hand away and sat up. "No. I can't do this now." I'd been dreading this moment. The night of his birthday had been a mistake. I saw that clearly now. I hadn't spent much time worrying about it though because I'd been preoccupied with my aunt's recovery. After a few days had passed and Alex hadn't mentioned it, I was hoping he never would and we could just pretend it never happened. Wishful thinking.

Alex rolled over onto his back. "Then when?"

I buried my face in my hands. There was no point putting off the conversation. It was inevitable. I looked up. "The night of your birthday was...an anomaly. You caught me at a weak moment. Us sleeping together is a bad idea. You know it as well as I do."

"No, I don't," he said, his voice somewhere between angry and confused. "But I'm just a dumb high school dropout, not a high-class lawyer like you."

"Oh, don't give me that shit. You know exactly why this is a bad idea. It's only going to make a confusing situation even more confusing."

"I'm not confused. I know exactly what I want."

"Fine, then I'm the only one who's confused."

"Why?" His voice softened. "You know I want you. I think you want me too. What's confusing about that?"

"It's not that simple."

"Sure it is." He reached for my hand and tried to pull me back down so I was lying flat on the bed.

I jerked my hand away from his and jumped up. "I said no! No means no, Alex."

At first, he just stared at me. Then his expression hardened and he pushed himself off the bed.

We drove back to my aunt's house in silence. Instead of parking in the driveway like he usually did, he pulled up to the curb and left the engine running. If this was a date, I could've gotten out of the car and never seen him again. But this wasn't a date. I had to somehow diffuse the tension between us.

"This isn't about you," I said. "You know that."

He didn't answer me.

"I just can't deal with this now on top of everything else. My aunt, the kids, Igor. The situation is way too complicated."

"Sure," he said, staring straight ahead.

"I don't want things to be awkward between us."

No response.

"Is there anything you want to say to me?"

"Can you get the fuck out of my car already?"

Chapter 26

"Surely you understand why his feelings are hurt," Dr. Rubenstein said at our next appointment. I'd seen Alex twice since he told me to get the fuck out of his car—when he'd picked up the kids from my aunt's house the next morning and when he'd dropped them off that night. He didn't speak to me either time. And we were driving back to LA together tonight. I was dreading it. Not just the two-hour ride, but all the days to come.

"We were never supposed to sleep together," I said. "This was always going to be a pretend relationship to keep Igor's men from hassling me. Even when we shared that hotel room in Oregon, he slept on the floor, which was his idea. If his feeling weren't hurt back then, why are they hurt now?"

"Because you opened the door to this. And now you're slamming it shut in his face."

"I didn't slam it shut. I just said I couldn't deal with it now. He knows I'm worried about my aunt and what's going to happen when Maria files for custody again, not to mention the entire situation with Igor. Maybe it's not the best time to embark on a new relationship."

"You're already in a relationship, Grace. Just not a sexual relationship."

"If we sleep together, it will make everything more complicated. You know that."

"I'm not the one you have to convince."

"You're telling me I have to convince Alex? When have I ever been able to convince Alex of anything?"

Dr. Rubenstein laughed. "I bet if he was sitting here now, he'd say the exact same thing about you."

"Exactly! All we do is argue. Agent Diaz told us once we sounded like his in-laws and they'd been unhappily married for years."

Dr. Rubenstein didn't respond.

"Well? Don't you think that's reason enough not to sleep with him?"

She shrugged. "I told you, I'm not the one you need to convince."

"And I just told you I can't convince Alex of anything."

"I wasn't referring to Alex. I was referring to you. Alex knows what he wants. You're the one who's on the fence."

"I'm not on the fence. I've made my decision. I'm not going to sleep with him."

"Okay," she said.

We sat in silence for a while until I finally said, "How come I don't feel any better? Usually when I make a decision about something I've been stressing over, I feel better. It's a relief just knowing it's settled once and for all."

"I think you just answered your own question."

I HUGGED MJ, Sofia, and my aunt, then my mom walked me to the front door. Alex was waiting for me in the car.

"I'll be back Thursday night," I said, "But if something

happens and you need me to come home sooner, just call me. I'm only two hours away."

"We'll be fine," my mom said, hugging me goodbye. "If I need help, I have MJ."

"You're sure?" I asked.

"I think I can hold down the fort for a few days without you. Go do what you need to do. We'll be here when you get back."

As expected, Alex didn't talk much on the drive to LA. I tried to engage him in conversation several times, but after receiving one-word responses I gave up and listened to the radio.

When we arrived at the house, I went to my bedroom and he went to his. I showered and changed into pajamas then wandered into the living room. Alex was sitting in the center of the couch with his feet up on the coffee table, watching a baseball game on TV and drinking a beer.

"Can I join you?" I asked.

"I thought you didn't like baseball," he said without looking away from the screen.

"I don't. I was just hoping for some company."

He slid over to the far end of the couch, leaving plenty of space for me.

I nodded to his beer bottle, which was almost empty. "You want another?" I asked.

"Sure," he said.

I walked into the kitchen and was relieved to see he'd cleaned while I was away. The last time I was here was the night of his birthday and I'd left a mess. I opened the refrigerator and stared at the cans of soda and bottles of beer. Then I spied the margarita mix in the side door and grabbed that instead. I searched the cabinets until I found tequila and margarita glasses. I was holding the lid on the blender while it made its high-pitched squeal when Alex wandered in.

"What are you doing?" he asked.

"Making margaritas. You want one?"

He shrugged. "Sure."

I pulled a second glass from the cabinet and salted the rim. Then I filled both glasses with frozen margarita and handed him one. I held up my glass, prepared to make a toast, when I realized I didn't know what to say. "What should we toast to? The last couple of weeks have pretty much sucked."

"To better days," Alex said.

"To better days," I agreed and clinked my glass against his.

I brought the pitcher to the kitchen table and sat down. Alex followed me, but neither one of us spoke. When we'd each drained half our glass, Alex topped them both off. It didn't take long for the alcohol to hit my blood stream. As soon as I felt my shoulders relax, I said, "I'm sorry if you feel like I led you on. That wasn't my intention. All this is just so much harder than I thought it would be."

I wanted to discuss it with him. We needed to hash this out and move on. But Alex just picked up his drink and walked back into the living room.

It was obvious he didn't want to talk to me, but I followed him anyway. "Aren't you going to say anything?"

Alex looked up at me from the couch, the baseball game still playing on the TV. "What do you want me to say?"

"I apologized. Can't you forgive me?"

"You're forgiven. Can I watch the game now?"

"Sure." I stomped back into the kitchen so I could brood alone.

Ten minutes later Alex wandered in.

"Commercial?" I asked.

"Refill." He poured more margarita into his glass.

I thought he'd leave again, but he didn't. He leaned his back against the kitchen counter and folded his arms across his chest.

"Here's what I don't get. You made me dinner, bought me a present, turned on a romantic movie—"

"The movie was your idea, not mine."

"But you agreed to watch it. And you'd seen it before, so you knew what it was about."

I couldn't argue with that.

He chuckled. "You know, I was actually afraid to kiss you."

"You were afraid of me? I find that hard to believe." There was no doubt he was physically stronger than me.

"I figured the odds were fifty-fifty you'd slap me across the face and tell me to fuck off. But you didn't."

"No, I didn't."

"So, you see how I might've thought you actually liked me."

"I do like you."

"Just not enough to sleep with me."

"It's not that I don't want to sleep with you." The margaritas were not helping the situation, because in this moment I very much wanted to sleep with Alex.

"Except you won't."

"Not won't. Shouldn't."

"I don't even know what that means."

I could blame it on the tequila coursing through my veins, but it wasn't the tequila. It was me. I just decided to do what I felt like doing instead of what I knew I should do. I set down my margarita glass and pushed away from the table. I stood before him defiant, with my arms folded across my chest. "You want to kiss me so bad, kiss me."

"Why?" he asked warily. "What are you going to do?"

"Kiss me and find out."

"Don't fuck with me, Grace. It won't end well for you."

"I'm not fucking with you. I've laid down the gauntlet. Are you going to pick it up or not?"

Chapter 27

I DIDN'T HAVE to ask twice. Alex grabbed me by the shoulders and kissed me, long and deep. At first, I continued to keep my arms folded across my chest, but it didn't take long before I was pulling his shirt over his head and he was tugging mine off too. We let our hands and our mouths roam freely and quickly consummated our relationship on the kitchen floor. This was the first time I'd ever come at exactly the same moment as the person I was with. It was explosive; the sense of relief exquisite.

Then we moved into my bedroom and took our time. After two more orgasms, I was spent.

"Can I ask you something?" I said as we laid side by side in my bed. Alex's chest was covered in a fine layer of perspiration, some of which had rubbed off onto me.

"Sure," he said.

"Why are you doing this?"

That was the first time I'd heard him give a genuine belly laugh. "Are you kidding? I've wanted to do this since the day I met you."

"Not this," I said. "I meant why are you helping me? I know you didn't want to. Agent Diaz told me he'd tried for years to get you to testify against the Russians and you refused. So why now? What did he promise you?"

"The same thing the FBI promises everyone who agrees to testify in a case like this. Witness Protection."

"But you could've gotten that anytime. What changed?"

He shrugged. "Seemed like the right time, I guess." Then he rolled over onto his side so his back was facing me. He yawned loudly then went silent, and I assumed he'd fallen asleep. I was starting to drift off too, when he suddenly said, "I was a lot like MJ when I was a kid. I got good grades, played sports, all the parents liked me."

I was afraid to speak. Afraid I might say the wrong thing and he'd clam up again. But I was equally afraid if I didn't speak, he might think I was sleeping, or worse, that I didn't care. "So what happened to change your trajectory?"

Alex let out a laugh and rolled over onto his back. "I love the way you talk."

"How do I talk?"

"With a lot of fancy words. And you make everything sound like a big project or some problem for you to fix."

From someone else I might've taken that as a compliment, but not the way Alex said it. "Sorry."

Alex turned to face me. "Don't apologize. I like your fancy words. And you're good at fixing things. I'm really grateful for what you've done for the kids."

"Anyone would've done the same."

"That's not true," he said, suddenly angry. "No one did anything for those kids. Not one person. Only you. And what you're doing now...I can't imagine anyone else taking on Igor. I think you're amazing."

I laughed. "No need to flatter me. You already got me into bed."

Alex rolled on top of me. "What if I said you could never leave, that I want this to last forever?"

"I would say I have to go to work in the morning and so do you, but there's a good chance of this happening again. Just not tonight. I'm a little sore."

"Sorry," he said and rolled off me.

"I'm not complaining." We may not have been compatible outside the bedroom, but we were definitely compatible inside it.

"Good," he said, clearly proud of himself.

I didn't want to have sex again, but I did want him to keep talking. "So you were telling me...what happened to change your trajectory?"

Alex chuckled and shook his head, then his smile disappeared. "My dad died when I was thirteen."

"I'm so sorry, Alex. That must've been horrible for you."

"For all of us. But I was with him. I watched him die."

"Oh my god."

Alex turned away from me and stared up at the ceiling. "We were driving home from my baseball game. My dad came to all my games. I was good. Really good. My parents were hoping I'd get a scholarship because there was no money for college. We were stopped at a red light when two cars came up on either side of us. My dad realized what was happening before I did. He pushed me down. Saved my life. The bullet smashed my window and hit him in the head."

"Jesus Christ."

"He didn't do nothing wrong. Didn't even know the guys. Just a bunch of gangbangers having a turf war."

"I'm so sorry, Alex. That is truly horrible."

"What's it called? Irony? He never even got a traffic ticket. Worked construction. That ain't easy money. My mom cleaned for rich people. But she couldn't pay the mortgage on that. We thought we were gonna lose the house."

"But you didn't," I said. "You still own it."

"Yes. And someday it'll belong to MJ and Sofia."

"What happened? How did your mom get the money?"

"She didn't. I did."

I stayed quiet and eventually Alex continued.

"At first, I was just a lookout. I'd let the guys know if the cops were around. But as I got older, Lucky gave me more responsibility."

"Lucky?"

"Carlos Lucky Lopez, your friendly neighborhood drug dealer. He got the nickname because a lot of guys around him got taken out, either by a bullet or by the cops, but somehow Lucky always managed to survive. Until he didn't. I was his number two when one of the Bloods finally got him. I took over when he was gone."

"So, you sort of fell into the drug business?"

"You could say that."

"But you stayed."

"Yeah, Grace, I stayed. I'm a high school dropout. What else was I supposed to do? Go work at McDonald's for minimum wage? Break my back in construction like my old man until somebody blows my brains out for no reason?"

I didn't respond because I didn't know what to say.

"If you want to know why I'm doing this," he continued, his voice still tinged with anger, "it's because I don't want MJ to end up like me. I want him to end up like you."

"I'd help MJ anyway. Sofia too. This isn't a quid pro quo."

"I know, but you wouldn't back off this thing with Igor. When Roberto came to me and told me he was thinking of letting you do this I told him he was nuts, that you both were. But he took a lot of heat when your husband died and he had to shut down his investigation. He wasn't gonna pass up a second chance. He wants to get Igor almost as much as you do."

"So you're doing this to help both of us?"

"No. I told you, I'm doing this for MJ and Sofia. So they can keep living with you. That's not gonna happen if you do something stupid and get yourself killed. Did you think Roberto was kidding when he said my job was to keep you alive?"

After a long pause, I said, "The kids may not get to stay with me anyway. Your sister's made no secret of wanting them back."

He sighed. "Yeah, I know."

"Janelle says it's going to happen. If Maria stays clean, the court will grant her custody again. There's nothing I can do to stop it."

Alex rolled over so his back was facing me. "It's late. Let's get some sleep."

THE NEXT MORNING, Igor and Sergey walked into the gallery ten minutes after I did. It made me wonder if they weren't watching the security cameras waiting for me to arrive. Only Igor joined me in the office. I knew Sergey was nearby, but as long as I didn't have to be alone with him, I was okay with that.

Igor took his usual spot on the couch, and I swallowed my anger and pasted a smile on my face.

"How's your aunt?" he asked.

"Getting better," I said, focusing on a spot on the wall behind his head so I didn't have to look at his face. "Thank you for the flowers, by the way."

He waved away my thanks. "You're behind on your invoices."

"I know. I'll get them out today."

"I need you to increase the retainers by ten percent each."

"Okay. Any particular reason?" I tried not to stare at the

pencil cup. I knew the recording pen was in there, but I had a hard time recognizing it since it looked exactly the same as the rest of the pens. I only knew which one held the recording device because it was heavier than the others. I hoped the battery hadn't died. I'd been at my aunt's house for the last two weeks so I hadn't been able to change it out.

"Because I told you to," Igor said and stood up. "I'll be back later with more files. Send out the invoices by the end of the day."

I didn't ask *or else what?* But I wondered.

Chapter 28

"DID you find anything useful in the files?" Agent Diaz asked a few days later. We were meeting alone at a Starbucks next to the freeway. I passed it on my way home to Santa Veneta.

"No, nothing. Was there anything useful on the pen?" I'd given it to Alex to pass on to him earlier in the week.

He shook his head.

"I don't think Igor trusts me."

"He trusts you. If he didn't, he'd put a bullet in your head."

I shivered involuntarily and pushed the thought from my mind. "Then why isn't he confiding in me? Except for the inflated invoices, it's all legitimate legal work."

"Igor hasn't survived this long by being sloppy. You need to be patient."

"I'm trying, but it's hard. I hate lying to everyone. And I feel like the lines are starting to blur."

He set down his coffee cup. "Has something happened?"

"No." Alex and I agreed to keep our relationship a secret. Ironically, the only people we were honest with were Igor and his crew since they already thought we were a couple, even before we'd slept together. "I just feel like I don't know who I am anymore."

"That happens sometimes," Agent Diaz said, "even to seasoned agents. Go home, Grace. Hug the kids. Tell your family you love them. It'll remind you why you're doing this."

It was a tight squeeze with all five of us at the kitchen table, but we were happy to have my aunt eating meals with us again, although my mom and I did all the cooking now. We were looking forward to the day when my aunt could climb the stairs so we could get rid of the hospital bed and convert her temporary bedroom back into a dining room.

"It's not a prom," MJ said, helping himself to more mashed potatoes. "Prom is only for juniors and seniors. It's just a dance."

"Fine, it's a dance," I said. "I can still take pictures, can't I?"

MJ rolled his eyes and my mother laughed. She was enjoying this argument way too much.

"Don't make any plans for after school tomorrow," I told him. "I'm taking you to buy a jacket."

"I have a jacket," MJ said.

"You are not going to a school dance in a hoodie. You need a blazer. And maybe a tie."

"I'm not wearing a tie," MJ said. "I'll look like a dork."

"Fine, no tie." I'd learned to choose my battles with MJ. "How about some new shoes?" He wore the same pair of sneakers every day. Every single day.

"No," he said through a mouthful of potatoes.

I turned to my mother, hoping for some words of wisdom, but she just shrugged. "Okay, you can wear your sneakers, but you're buying Olivia a corsage. That's my final offer."

MJ asked, "What's a corsage?"

. . .

Alex drove up to Santa Veneta on Saturday because I asked him to. We told my mom and my aunt it was because he wanted to visit Maria, which was true. But it wasn't the real reason I'd asked him to come. I wanted him to have the sex talk with MJ before the dance tonight. MJ insisted he and Olivia were just going together as friends, but even if that was true, I knew how quickly things could change.

I told my mom and my aunt I had errands to run, then I drove over to my house to meet Alex for a quickie. It was as if now that we'd finally slept together, the dam had broken. We couldn't keep our hands off each other. I didn't even realize until afterward that this was the first time I'd had sex in this bed with anyone but Jonah. The weird part was that it wasn't weird at all.

After we were both satiated, I reminded Alex again that sex was just a bonus. He was here to talk to MJ.

"He's a sixteen-year-old boy. Don't you think he already knows about sex?"

I said, "I'm sure he knows the mechanics of it. But I'm not confident anyone has explained to him the importance of using protection. Can you please share that information and buy him a box of condoms? I think he'll be more open to having that conversation with you than with me."

Alex laughed. "I cannot even imagine talking to my mother about sex."

"Does that mean it was your father who taught you about the birds and the bees? Or did you learn it all from watching porn?"

"I'm not going to answer that question."

"Smart man," I said. "A good defendant knows when to shut his mouth."

Alex rolled over onto his side and started tracing circles around my belly button with the tip of his finger. I knew where he was headed with this move—he'd used it on me before—but I was happy with the destination. "Since we're talking about it" he asked, widening his circle, "what kind of protection are you using?"

I placed my hand over his to stop it from moving. "Why would I be using protection? You're the one who can't have kids."

"Where did you get that idea?"

"From you! Don't you remember that day we took Sofia and Tim and Richard's other foster kids to the park and you shredded their baby carrier for no earthly reason? I asked you if you had any children and you said no, and I said accidents happen, and you said not to you. You told me you were one hundred percent sure you couldn't have any."

"I didn't say I *couldn't* have any, I said I *didn't* have any."

"That is *not* what you said."

"It is," he said. "And why are you mad at me? Isn't not getting pregnant the girl's responsibility?"

I thought my head was going to explode. "I'm going to pretend you did not just say that to me," I said, straining to keep my voice even. "And you better never say that to MJ." I slid out of bed and pulled on my panties. "It takes two people to make a baby, Alex, so it's both people's responsibility. Now get your ass up."

"Why?" he asked, looking quite comfortable laying on Jonah's pillow with his hands behind his head.

"Because we're going to the drugstore."

"Now?"

"Yes, now." I grabbed his underwear off the floor and threw it at him. "You need to buy condoms and I'm buying a morning-after pill."

Chapter 29

WE TOOK pictures with MJ at my aunt's house first. Then my mom stayed with my aunt and Alex drove the four of us—me, him, MJ, and Sofia—to Olivia's house.

"Whoa," Alex said when the metal gate slid open and he continued up the long driveway. "This reminds me of Igor's house."

I'd never been to Igor's house. I'd never been invited. But I knew Alex went there frequently. *Less guns, I imagine,* I thought but didn't say.

Alex parked in front of the three-car garage and I handed MJ the corsage of pink roses. He looked so grownup in his navy blazer I couldn't help but beam at him.

"So do I, like, pin it on her?" he asked.

An image of MJ awkwardly trying to pin flowers onto Olivia's chest flashed through my mind. "No, just hand it to her. It has a wristband."

The four of us plus the housekeeper and Olivia's mother stood in the foyer. At first, I thought it was rude of Olivia's mother not to invite us inside to sit down, but when Olivia appeared at the top of the sweeping staircase, I understood. She wanted her grand entrance.

"Holy shit," Alex whispered.

"She's sixteen," I whispered back. "Whatever you're thinking, stop."

Olivia's mother must've taken Olivia to have her hair and makeup done because the coltish sixteen-year-old looked like a supermodel. Her pink hair was blonde again and framed her face in long beachy waves, her eyes were dusted with glitter, her lips and cheeks were dewy, and the hem of her body-hugging dress was closer to her vagina than her knees. My mother never would've let me leave the house in a dress that short, but Claire Baylor smiled up at her daughter as she clomped down the stairs in silver, five-inch heels. She hadn't mastered the catwalk yet.

MJ and Olivia hugged awkwardly then we all moved outside to take pictures. Most of the photos we snapped were of the two of them, but Olivia's mother insisted on taking a picture of me and Alex with MJ and Sofia.

"But you're such a cute family!" she said when I protested. It was easier to smile and go along with it than correct her.

We'd offered to drive MJ and Olivia to the dance and pick them up at the end of the night, but Olivia's mother had already booked an Uber Black, and she was fine paying the driver extra to make two stops on the way home. Alex dropped off me and Sofia at my aunt's house before returning to LA.

I SPENT two more nights in Santa Veneta, then drove down to LA too. When I arrived home Alex was in the kitchen cooking dinner —something with a lot of garlic by the scent of it. I couldn't pinpoint the moment when I'd stopped thinking of it as "the house in LA" and started thinking of it as "home," but it had happened.

Alex turned down the heat on whatever he was cooking and gave me a long, deep kiss.

"I hope you bought extra condoms," I said when we came up for air.

"I thought you were going to the doctor."

I told Alex I was going back on the pill, but I needed a prescription. "I tried. Her first available appointment isn't until the end of August. That means you're using a condom until then."

Alex groaned.

"If you don't want to use them, we can always go back to being roommates."

"Or we could do other things."

"We could." I couldn't keep the smile off my face. Oral sex was one area where Alex really excelled, and he knew it.

Alex shut off the stove and moved the frying pan to a cool burner. Then he lifted me off the ground and threw me over his shoulder as if I was a giant sack of rice.

"What the hell are you doing?" I cried.

"You first. Dinner later."

We used a lot of condoms the next two weeks.

The school year ended on a Friday. The kids spent Saturday with Maria, and on Sunday night I packed suitcases for both of them and drove us down to LA. Sofia was excited to go to camp and spend the summer with her uncle. MJ was miserable he was being forced to leave his friends.

"You can get a job," I said as we drove south on the 101. "I looked online and there are still plenty of openings for camp counselors. One of the listings was for someone to help coach boys' basketball. You could do that, right?"

MJ shot me side eye from the passenger seat.

"And your uncle's going to teach you to drive this summer. That's exciting."

I thought the idea of getting to drive Alex's BMW would bring a smile to MJ's face, but he didn't even look up from his phone.

"Did I tell you the house has a pool? That'll be fun."

"Maybe if I knew how to swim," MJ said.

"You don't know how to swim? But you go in the ocean." I'd seen him wade into the water at the beach last summer.

"Not to swim," he said. "Just to mess around."

I looked into the rearview mirror. "Sofia, do you know how to swim?"

"No," she said, "but I want to."

"Okay, then we'll put that on our list for summer too."

Alex was waiting for us at the house when we arrived. Sofia jumped into his outstretched arms, but MJ walked right past him and headed for the living room. There was a baseball game playing on the television, but MJ snatched the remote off the coffee table and pulled up the on-screen channel guide.

"I was watching that," Alex said.

MJ ignored him and kept scrolling through the listings.

Alex grabbed the remote from MJ's hand and clicked back over to the baseball game. "You need to learn some respect, *hijo*."

"You're not my father," MJ shouted.

I'd seen Alex angry before, usually at me, but I'd never seen him like this. He grabbed MJ under the arm and literally dragged him out the front door of the house.

I handed Sofia her iPad and said, "Wait here." Then I ran outside too. I found Alex and MJ in the driveway. Alex had pinned MJ to the hood of his car.

"Jesus, Alex, what the hell are you doing? It's just a game. You can record them all and watch them whenever you want."

"This is not about the game," he said. "This kid needs to show some respect."

MJ rolled his eyes.

Alex grabbed MJ by the collar and pulled him upright. "I swear, *hijo*, you do that one more time and you won't be able to sit for a week."

"You can't hit him!" I shouted.

"The hell I can't," Alex said. Then he dragged MJ to the passenger side of the car and pushed him into the seat. "We're gonna have a talk, just you and me," he said before he slammed the door shut. Then he walked around to the driver's side door and wrenched it open.

I grabbed the door frame so he couldn't leave. "Alex, listen to me. You cannot hit him. People don't do that anymore. Seriously. It's not allowed. You'll be the one who ends up in trouble."

Alex mumbled something in Spanish then pushed my hand away before he slammed the door shut. Moments later the car's engine rumbled to life and Alex squealed out of the driveway and sped off down the street.

I went back inside and found Sofia where I'd left her on a chair in the living room. I gave her a tour of the house and let her choose which bedroom would be hers for the summer, although it was obvious which one she'd want. The owner of the house had already decorated one of the rooms with a child in mind. There was a twin bed covered in a colorful duvet, a cloth tent set up in the corner, and a combination bookcase/toy bin just waiting to be filled with her treasures.

I unpacked Sofia's clothes while she placed her toys and stuffed animals on the shelves. When we'd finished, she asked when MJ and Uncle Alex would be back. I told her I didn't know and took her out for ice cream to distract her.

By the time we returned, Alex's car was in the driveway. It

was so late I decided Sofia could skip a bath tonight. I helped her into her pajamas, read her one book, then turned out the light.

I found Alex in the living room watching the baseball game. "Where's MJ?" I asked.

Alex shrugged.

I sat down on the chair across from him and paused the TV. "We need to have a conversation about your behavior."

"*My* behavior?" Alex picked up the remote and un-paused the game. "That kid has an attitude problem," he said, staring at the television.

"He's a teenager. That's how they are."

"That's not how I was."

"You can't compare your childhood to his. At his age you were supporting your family."

Alex folded his arms across his chest and silently fumed.

I paused the TV again and moved to the couch. "Alex, this is what you wanted. It's why you're willing to give up everything and go into Witness Protection. It's so MJ and Sofia can have the kind of life you didn't get." I gently placed my hand on his arm. "But it's not too late for you either, you know."

He slapped my hand away. "I'm not one of your projects, Grace. You can't fix me." Then he stomped out of the house, slamming the front door shut behind him. A minute later I heard his car roar to life and his tires squeal out of the driveway.

Chapter 30

THE BEDROOM DOOR WAS SHUT, but I could see light peeking from underneath so I knocked. "It's me," I said.

No answer.

"I just want to talk to you."

No answer.

"Please. Your uncle left. It's only me."

I heard shuffling, then MJ cracked open the bedroom door. His eyes were bloodshot and watery as if he'd been crying, but I didn't see any bruises. He returned to the bed and laid down on his side with his back to me. I sat down next to him and placed my hand on his knee.

"So good talk with your uncle then?" I asked.

MJ chuckled and I did too.

"I know he can be a jerk sometimes, but he really does love you and wants what's best for you."

No response.

"He's sacrificing a lot for you."

"No, he's not! He's not doing anything."

"You're wrong, MJ. There are things going on you don't know about. Things he can't tell you."

MJ rolled over onto his back. "Like what?"

"I can't tell you either."

He turned and faced the wall again. "He ruined everything! I shouldn't even be here. I should be in Santa Veneta with my friends."

"Look at me, MJ." But he refused to turn around, so I talked to his back instead. "You cannot blame any of this on your uncle. It was *my* idea for you and Sofia to spend the summer in LA, not his. Aunt Maddy can't take care of you and Sofia right now. You know that."

"So she sent us away again?"

"No! I swear to you she never said a word. This was all my idea. And it's just for the summer. I promise. We're all moving back to Santa Veneta when school starts again in the fall."

MJ rolled onto his back and looked up at me. "Uncle Alex too?"

"No. Just you, me, and Sofia. But your uncle can come and visit if he wants."

MJ stared at me. "What's going on with you and him?"

"What do you mean?"

"Are you guys, like, together now? Is that why we're all here?"

I truly hated lying to him, but Alex and I had decided the less the kids knew about any of this, the better. "MJ, you can't be serious. Do you honestly think I would date your uncle? C'mon, you're smarter than that. The house has four bedrooms, one for each of us."

MJ smiled. "So you're not doing it?"

"Are you and Olivia doing it?" I shot back.

MJ blushed. "We're hanging out."

"Hanging out? Is that like dating?" MJ rolled his eyes and I laughed.

Then I recalled my conversation with Alex. "Just promise

me if you are doing it with Olivia or anyone else, you will use protection. Because contrary to what you may have heard, it's not just the girl's responsibility. Girls don't get pregnant on their own. They need a boy for that."

MJ reached behind him for one of his pillows and held it over his face. "Please go."

"Okay, I get it. You don't want to talk to me about the sex stuff. I just wanted you to know I'm here for you, whatever you need, and that includes condoms."

"Grace!"

I laughed. "Okay, okay, I'm leaving."

I made it as far as the bedroom door when MJ lifted the pillow from his face. "Love you, Lawyer-Mom," he mumbled.

"Love you too," I said and shut the door behind me.

I called Agent Diaz the next morning and insisted we meet.

Chapter 31

AGENT DIAZ SLID into the seat across from me at the Boba shop near his office. "What's the emergency? Did something happen?"

"No, everything's fine," I replied. "I just wanted to tell you I've made a decision. I'm going back to Santa Veneta at the end of the summer."

"I thought Igor wanted you in LA."

"He does."

Agent Diaz shook his head. "Then I don't understand."

"I can't do this anymore."

"Do what? Work for Igor?"

"All of it. The kids are going back to Santa Veneta in the fall, and I'm going with them. I need to be there for them."

"I thought their mother was suing for custody."

"She is, but I'm going back. I promised MJ."

Agent Diaz took a sip of his tea and stared at me. "You know what that means, don't you? The only reason the bureau agreed to reopen this investigation is because you agreed to be a confidential informant. You leave and the whole thing gets shut down again."

"Why? You still have Alex? Why do you need me too? Igor never tells me anything anyway."

"He will," he said. "You have to give it time."

"I'm giving it until the end of the summer. When school starts again, I'm leaving."

MJ GOT a job as a counselor at the same summer camp Sofia attended, which made life a lot easier for me. It meant I could drop them both off and pick them both up together instead of driving from one end of LA to the other every morning and afternoon. Occasionally, Alex dropped them off or picked them up if I couldn't, but the default seemed to be it was my responsibility and he helped out when he could.

Alex and I hadn't had sex once since the kids moved in. Part of it was now that MJ and Sofia were living with us, Alex slept in his own bedroom again. And part of it was I'd shifted my schedule to accommodate the kids' schedule, so we hardly saw each other anymore. Alex was rarely awake when the kids and I left the house in the morning, and he often didn't arrive home until late in the evening after the kids and I had gone to bed. Maybe if I'd stayed in LA on weekends, we would've spent time together, but I always drove the kids up to Santa Veneta to see their mother.

By July Maria had finally saved enough money from her waitressing job that she could afford to move out of the halfway house and into her own apartment. Her new place was only a few blocks away from where she used to live with the kids, which meant it was near my office too. Since I hadn't been there in weeks, I decided to swing by after I dropped the kids off Saturday morning. As I pulled into the strip mall parking lot, I spotted Mike Murphy across the street and we waved to each other.

I was sitting at my desk going through a stack of mail when I heard the bell on the door tinkle. A few seconds later Mike Murphy stood in my doorway.

"I haven't seen you in a while," he said.

"I know." I motioned for him to sit. "I'm doing a lot of work for a client in LA and he prefers to meet face-to-face, so I spend a lot of time down there now. How are things here?"

Mike nodded, which I took to mean everything was fine. "I've been wanting to talk to you."

"About?"

"This place," he said and glanced around my office.

"You got my rent check, right?" I'd mailed it this month instead of dropping it off in-person like I usually did.

He nodded again. "Yup. Seems a shame to keep paying rent for a place you're never at."

He was right, but I liked knowing the office was here waiting for me. I'd start coming again in the fall when I moved back.

"The thing is," he continued, "You need to move out."

Chapter 32

"You're evicting me!" I said. "But I pay my rent on time every month."

"Not just you," Mike Murphy said. "All the tenants."

"Why? Don't you want the income?"

He sighed and leaned back in his chair. "There's this developer. He's been hounding me for months. Wants to tear this place down and build something new. Retail on the bottom with apartments on top. I've been saying no, but I had a health scare recently and—"

"Oh no. Are you okay?" He didn't look ill.

"Yeah, I'm fine. But my kids have been after me to retire for a while now."

"You're selling the shop too?"

"Eventually. One of the guys who works for me wants to buy it, but he needs to scrape together the money first. Right now, I'm just selling this place."

I didn't love this office, but it was better than looking for a new one. Now I'd have no choice. "What will you do when you retire? Are you going to stay in the area?"

"I don't know yet," he said. "Still figuring it out."

"Well, congratulations, I guess."

"Thanks," he said and stood up. "If you could have your stuff out by the end of the month, I'd appreciate it."

I left my office and returned to my aunt's house, but neither she nor my mother was there. Then I remembered my mother mentioned my aunt had a physical therapy appointment this morning and figured that's where they must be. I had just sat down at the kitchen table with a cup of coffee and a slice of toast when my phone rang. It was Janelle's name on the caller ID and I panicked. Since we'd ended our law firm partnership, Janelle only ever called when she had news about Maria and the kids—and that news was rarely good.

"Is everything okay?" I asked.

"As far as I know," she said. "Why? Did something happen?"

I let out a breath. "No, I just thought...never mind. How are you? How's firm life?"

"Good," she said. "Turns out I like making money."

I laughed. "Yeah, that part is nice," I said, thinking of the wad of cash Igor handed me every week. I didn't get to keep all of it, but I kept more of it than I had when I worked for legitimate clients.

"How about you?" she asked. "How's it going with the new client?"

MJ must've told her. I wanted to get us off that topic as quickly as possible. "All good. What's the latest with Maria's custody suit?"

Janelle sighed. "You're not gonna like it."

I sighed too. Apparently, it was going to be one of those days.

. . .

None of us saw much of MJ over the weekend. He spent Saturday night "hanging out" with Olivia, and Sunday with his friends. But Sofia and I had plenty of fun without him. We baked cookies with my mom and aunt, binge-watched princess movies, and on Sunday the four of us went to a salon for mani-pedis.

I waited until after dinner on Sunday to start the drive back to LA. I helped Sofia with her bath and had her change into pajamas before we left my aunt's house, figuring she would fall asleep in the car on the way home, and she did. To my surprise, Alex was waiting for us when we arrived. He met us in the driveway and transferred Sofia to her bed without waking her, then carried our bags inside. MJ went directly to his bedroom and shut the door. I wandered into the kitchen to find something cold to drink.

Alex appeared next to me while I was scanning the contents of the refrigerator. He must've grocery shopped over the weekend because it was much fuller than when we'd left Friday night. "How was your weekend?" he asked.

"Good," I said as I popped open a can of raspberry seltzer. "Yours?"

He slid onto one of the barstools at the kitchen island. "Lonely." My shock must've registered on my face because he asked, "Why so surprised?"

I sat down on the barstool next to him. "I feel like I've hardly seen you the last couple of weeks. I was starting to think maybe you were avoiding me."

He shook his head. "No...work stuff."

"You want to talk about it?" I asked.

"I don't think you want to hear about it."

He was undoubtedly right. Alex knew I didn't like to know details about what he actually did for a living. It made it much harder for me to pretend he was someone other than who he was. Then I thought about that scene from *The Godfather* where Michael Corleone says, *Don't ask me about my business, Kay*, and I laughed. I felt like a mob wife. I knew exactly how it happened, but it was still incomprehensible to me.

"What's so funny?" Alex asked.

"Nothing," I said. "If you missed us so much, why didn't you come up to Santa Veneta? You knew where we were."

Alex didn't answer me.

"I should unpack," I said and hopped off my barstool. But before I could leave, Alex grabbed my hand.

"Don't go." He pulled me toward him and placed on hand on my ass while the other cupped my breast.

My desire flared, but I pulled away. "Not now," I whispered. "MJ's still awake."

"I don't give a fuck." Then he grabbed my hand and pulled me into the laundry room, slamming the door shut behind us.

"What if he hears," I protested.

"Don't care," Alex said as he pulled my shorts and underwear down in one swift movement. Then he knelt down in front of me and I no longer cared either.

I MADE Alex wait until I was sure MJ had fallen asleep before I let him join me in my bedroom, which was at the end of the hall and farthest from the kids' bedrooms. After we'd had our fill of each other, I told Alex about the latest with Maria.

"I'll talk to her," he said.

"You can talk to her all you want but it's not going to do any good. They're her kids, and she wants them back."

He sighed. "I have bad news too. Do you want to hear it?"

Not really, but I still said, "Yes."

"Something's up with Igor. He's acting strange."

"Do you think he suspects?"

"No, but I think trouble's brewing. He cancelled last Thursday night, and that's never happened before."

"Cancelled what?" I asked.

"Nothing. Just this thing he has for the guys. Maybe it's good the FBI's shutting us down."

I bolted upright. "What do you mean the FBI's shutting us down?"

Alex pushed up onto his elbow. "Roberto told me you pulled the plug. He said you didn't want to work for Igor anymore."

"I don't, but I'm not quitting. Not yet anyway. All I told him was I had to go back to Santa Veneta at the end of the summer. We still have two more months."

"That's not a lot of time."

"Because we're moving too slow. We can't just sit around waiting for something to happen. We have to make it happen."

At first, Alex was quiet. Then he said, "Listen to me, Grace. You need to let me handle this. Whatever you're thinking of doing, don't."

"If you think I'm going to walk away from this with nothing, think again. One way or another, Igor's going down."

Chapter 33

THE NEXT MORNING I waited for Igor and Sergey to show up at the gallery ten minutes after I arrived like they usually did. When they still hadn't come after half an hour, I decided it was time to do a little snooping. The alarm always beeped twice whenever anyone entered the building. That would give me enough warning to return to my desk.

I stared at the filing cabinets lined up against the wall. I still didn't know what was inside them. Alex was concerned the office might have hidden cameras, but I'd looked everywhere and hadn't found any. And we were running out of time. I decided it was worth the risk.

I pulled the handles on all three filing cabinets. Of course, they were locked. They were simple locks installed by the manufacturer and were probably easy to pick if you knew how, but I didn't. I spent a few minutes online watching a "how to pick a lock" video then gave up and searched for a key. I finally found the key ring buried at the bottom of a container filled with paper clips that had been sitting inside the top desk drawer since the day I arrived. It wasn't a bad hiding place. It would've taken me years to use that many paper clips.

When I unlocked the first file cabinet, I was shocked—not by any incriminating evidence but by the mess. Instead of neatly hanging file folders arranged in alphabetical order, it was a dumping ground for random stacks of papers. It would take me forever to sort this out.

Then I heard the alarm beep twice and I slammed the cabinet shut. I was sitting at my desk before Igor walked in.

"What are you doing?" he asked.

"Moving assets like you asked me to," I said, minimizing the document I had open on my computer screen. "No good morning?"

Igor sat down heavily on the couch. "Not so good morning."

"You look stressed."

Igor rubbed his eyes with the heels of his hand. "Yes. Much going on. I need you to send out the invoices early this month."

"Sure, no problem." I stared at Igor. The usual mix of rage and revulsion that roiled my stomach whenever I saw him was replaced with fear. I knew what I needed to say, but I was having a hard time forcing the words out. *Feel the fear and do it anyway.* It was Jonah's voice in my head. I took a deep breath to try to slow my heartbeat and said, "Is there anything else I can do for you? Maybe I can help alleviate some of the stress."

Igor stared at me in confusion. "You're not with Alex anymore?"

Oh shit. "No, no, no, that's not what I meant. Alex and I are still very much together. I was asking if there was anything I could do for you workwise. I feel like you're not really utilizing all of my skills. I'd like to take on more responsibility. Maybe it'll take some of the pressure off you."

"What did you have in mind?" he asked.

"I don't know. You've only given me insight into a small slice of your business. If I knew more about your operation, maybe I could help."

Igor stared at me. "Why you want to do this?"

I thought back to my conversation with Janelle. "For the money, of course. Isn't that why we all do this?"

"I pay you well," Igor said.

I swallowed hard. "You do. But, as you know, my aunt recently had a stroke. She'd like to retire, she *needs* to retire, but she can't afford to. I'd like to be in a position to help her out financially."

Igor continued to stare at me, lips sealed.

I needed to up the ante. "And Alex and I are thinking of starting a family. You know how expensive children can be."

Igor chuckled. "Yes, Mischa's very expensive."

"I think we could help each other out, that's all."

I tried to keep my expression neutral as Igor considered my offer. I prayed he couldn't hear my heart pounding from the other side of the room.

"I'll think about it," he finally said and stood up. "Get me the invoices by the end of the day."

"Absolutely."

I WAS SURPRISED to see Alex's car in the driveway when I returned home that evening with the kids. Alex was never home this early. Maybe reconnecting last night had a positive effect. Maybe he would start spending more time with the kids in the evening, and me after they'd gone to bed. But as soon as we walked into the house and I saw Alex's face, I knew I was mistaken. He gave me an icy stare. MJ noticed too. He glanced from Alex to me then grabbed Sofia's hand. "C'mon, let's go practice our swimming."

"Stay in the shallow end," I called out to MJ as he hustled Sofia out the sliding glass door to the patio.

Alex motioned for me to follow him into his bedroom,

which faced the front of the house. As soon as we were inside the room, he slammed the door shut behind me and started yelling. "What the fuck were you thinking? I told you not to do anything."

I wasn't one hundred percent sure he was referring to my conversation with Igor this morning, but I assumed. "I told you I wasn't walking away from this with nothing. Somebody had to do something."

His fists were clenched and his arms were pinned to his sides. When he spoke again his voice was low, which was even scarier than when he was shouting at me. "I said I'd handle it."

"Well, I decided to handle it myself."

I saw his fist coming and I ducked, although I didn't think he was aiming for me. Or maybe that's just what I wanted to believe. He punched a hole in the wall next to where my head had been.

"You need to calm down," I said.

One fist was still clenched. With the other hand he shook his finger in front of my face. "No. You need to do what I tell you to do. Tomorrow morning you're going to tell Igor you changed your mind."

"I don't think so," I said and turned to leave the room. That's when Alex grabbed me by the arm and slammed me against the wall. I could feel the tears stinging my eyes, but I held them back. When I spoke, my voice was as low as his. "Let go of me right this second, Alex, or I will walk out of this house and you will never see me or the kids again."

He held me a few seconds longer, then let me go.

I wrenched open the bedroom door, stopped, and turned around. "I'm going to forgive you for this because I have to. I can't do this alone. But do not *ever* touch me again." Then I grabbed my purse and keys off the entry table and ran out of the house.

Chapter 34

"I WAS SURPRISED to get your call," Jake said as we hugged hello outside the small Italian restaurant in Westwood Village.

Seeing him again gave me a chill like it always did because he looked so much like Jonah, but I shook it off. "It's been a while," I said, hugging him back.

He stepped back and held me at arm's length, studying my face. "Are you okay?"

I'd fixed my makeup in the car so it wouldn't be obvious I'd been crying, but maybe I hadn't done as good of a job as I thought. "Yes, fine. I just wanted to see a friendly face."

"Is that what I am now?" he asked. "Because that's not what you said to me the last time we saw each other."

I let out a small laugh and the tears came. "Well, you'd just told me you were responsible for Jonah and Amelia's death. How was I supposed to take that news?"

"Fair enough," he said. Then he put his arm around my shoulder and led me inside the restaurant.

As soon as we were seated, I went to the ladies room to fix my makeup again. When I returned to the table, I found two glasses of red wine. Jake said, "I thought you could use a drink."

I picked up the glass and stared at it. "You didn't spike it, did you?"

"Damn, I knew I forgot something," he said, and we both laughed. Then he reached across the table and gave my free hand a comforting squeeze.

I squeezed back. "Thanks for meeting me tonight. I just... needed a break."

"Of course," he said. "We're still family, aren't we?"

I nodded and changed the subject before I started bawling again. "What's going on with you?"

"Oh, you know. Can't talk about it. What's going on with you?" he asked.

"Same," I said and we both laughed again. Then I told him about my aunt's stroke and that MJ, Sofia, and I were spending the summer in LA, omitting any mention of Alex. When I finished talking, Jake told me he'd met someone.

"Is it serious?" I asked.

He shrugged. "Could be."

"Wow. Maybe all that diamond research you did will come in handy."

Jake smiled. "You never know." Then he turned thoughtful again. "It's hard, isn't it?"

"God, yes," I said, fighting back tears. "It's so much harder than I thought it would be. I think it may be the hardest thing I've ever done. And the lying is the worst part."

Jake picked up his wine glass and twirled it absentmindedly. "If the lying is the worst of it, then you've gotten off easy."

I STRETCHED out my dinner with Jake as long as I could, but when the waiter turned on the vacuum cleaner, I knew we had to go.

"Do you want a nightcap?" Jake asked as he walked me to my car. "Or maybe just a place to sleep?"

I shook my head. I had to go home eventually and putting it off wasn't going to make it any easier. I hugged Jake goodbye and promised to keep in touch. Then I climbed into my SUV and drove back to Hollywood.

Alex's car was parked in the driveway, but the house was dark. I unlocked the front door and tiptoed down the hallway to my bedroom, where I quickly undressed and slipped into bed. I thought I'd gotten lucky; it appeared everyone was asleep. So I was startled by the light knock on my bedroom door.

I assumed it was Alex coming to apologize. "Not now. We'll talk in the morning."

"Oh, okay." But it wasn't Alex's voice, it was MJ's.

I jumped out of bed and hurried to the door. When I opened it, I found a barefoot MJ in pajama bottoms and a T-shirt. "Is everything okay?" I asked.

"Yeah, I just wanted to make sure you were alright."

"I'm fine." I glanced at the glowing red numbers on the digital clock next to my bed. It was two minutes past midnight. "It's late. Why are you still awake?"

He shrugged. "Couldn't sleep. Uncle Alex wouldn't tell me where you went."

"He didn't know. I didn't tell him. If you were worried, why didn't you just text me?"

"He took my phone away. We had a fight after you left."

I mumbled a few curse words and promised to get him his phone back in the morning. "Do you remember my brother-in-law Jake? You met him that first night at my aunt's house. We had dinner tonight."

"You didn't tell my uncle?"

"No, I...left in a hurry."

"But you're okay? Everything's okay now?"

"Yes," I said. "Everything's fine. Now go get some sleep."

The next morning Alex strode into the kitchen while the kids and I were having breakfast. He placed MJ's phone on the counter without saying a word to him, and poured himself a cup of coffee.

"Do you want something to eat?" I asked.

"No," he said. "I'm going to take a shower." He left with his coffee cup.

I thought perhaps Alex's plan was to pretend that what happened between us last night had never happened. It might work if we kept our interactions to a minimum and didn't spend any time alone. So I was surprised when Alex showed up at the gallery shortly after noon.

"You need to come with me," he said without even a hello.

"I can't. I have work to do." The truth was I didn't want to be alone with Alex. Not now and maybe not ever. The physical attraction I'd felt for him had fizzled. Fear was not an aphrodisiac, at least not for me.

"I'm not the one who's asking. Igor is."

"Why didn't he ask me himself?"

Alex clenched his fists, and I sensed his struggle to stay calm. "You know that's not how this works. I'll be in the car." He turned and walked out of the gallery.

I knew if Igor summoned me, I had to go. Turning down Igor's request wasn't an option. I pulled my purse out of my desk drawer and grabbed my suit jacket off the back of my chair and joined Alex in his car. I hadn't even buckled my seatbelt yet when Alex squealed out of the parking lot. "You got what you wanted. I hope you're happy."

"And what is it exactly you think I want?"

Alex ran a red light, forcing another driver to slam on his

brakes to avoid hitting us. I could see the guy yelling at us through his windshield, but Alex ignored him and kept his ire trained on me. "Congratulations. You're now in the drug business."

"Wasn't I already in the drug business?" I knew I was laundering Igor's drug money even if I couldn't prove it.

"Not like you are now. Shit's about to get real."

Chapter 35

WE WOUND through the hills north of Sunset Boulevard in silence. Eventually, Alex stopped in front of a gated driveway, but instead of the usual intercom, there was a wooden hut with a heavily tattooed man inside. He and Alex nodded at each other, then the gate slid open. Alex drove up the steep incline and parked on the edge of a circular driveway where several other expensive cars were already parked, including Mischa's orange Lamborghini.

"Is this Mischa's house?" I asked.

"Igor's," Alex replied. "Mischa stays here too on the nights he's not fucking some boy in West Hollywood, but we don't talk about that."

Igor lived on a spectacular estate with an Olympic-size swimming pool, a tennis court, a putting green, a koi pond, and who knew how many bedrooms and bathrooms. The house was impressive based solely on its size, but too ornately decorated for my taste. I preferred clean lines and a lot less gilt.

The maid led us inside, but Alex knew his way around the house. I followed him through the first-floor rooms and out to a patio where Igor, Sergey, Mischa, and two other men I'd never seen before were gathered around a large round table in the shade. From the platters of food, I assumed they were eating lunch.

Igor waved us over. "Alex, Grace, join us."

I took the seat next to Mischa and Alex sat on my other side. The maid brought us each a steaming plate filled with what looked like some kind of stew over egg noodles. In the center of the table were trays filled with cucumbers, radishes, and sour cream, but they went untouched.

"Beef Stroganoff," Igor said, stabbing a chunk of meat on his plate. "Anya's is even better than my mother's."

The maid smiled at Igor. He said something to her in Russian and she returned to the house.

I took a small bite of the meat. I'd never eaten beef stroganoff before, but I liked it.

"Ekatarina's shopping," Igor said. "You'll meet her next time."

"The evil stepmother," Mischa stage whispered before I could ask. Then he glanced at Igor, who was not smiling. "Just kidding. She's fine."

"Very fine," Igor said and all the men at the table except for Mischa laughed.

When everyone had finished eating, Anya cleared the dishes and brought out an assortment of pastries. Everyone except for Alex drank tea, so I did too. Anya didn't offer coffee. Then Igor poured himself a glass of vodka and passed the bottle around. I didn't want any, but Mischa poured a splash into my glass before I could stop him. When Igor lifted his glass for a toast, I hoisted mine too. He spoke in Russian first, then turned to me. "Welcome to the organization, Grace."

Everyone downed their vodka except for me.

"Sorry?" I said.

"I'm taking you up on your offer," Igor said as he poured

himself another drink. He raised his glass again. "To your health."

This time when everyone drank, I did too.

Igor set down his glass. "We'll talk tomorrow. But you and Alex should get married right away."

"Excuse me?" I must've misunderstood.

Igor stared at me. "You're good lawyer. I shouldn't have to explain. You can't testify against each other if you're married. Plus, you want baby. You should be married first."

I glanced at Alex, but his expression was inscrutable. I turned back to Igor. "Yes, but we need to wait until my aunt recovers. I want her to be at my wedding. I want all my family to be there."

"You want big wedding?" Igor said. "You can get married here. Plenty of room." He waved at the expansive lawn. "Ekaterina can help you plan. She loves parties."

I glanced at Alex again. His jaw was clenched and he continued to stare straight ahead. Obviously, I was on my own. "That's very kind of you, Igor, but I don't want a big wedding. I've always imagined having a small ceremony with just my family and a few close friends." A memory flashed through my mind—Jonah and I dancing together for the first time as husband and wife in the ballroom at my parent's country club in front of two hundred guests—and I banished it. "But I think we're getting ahead of ourselves. Alex hasn't even bought me a ring yet." I held up my left hand and wiggled my unadorned fingers.

"You will have your ring soon," Igor said. "Trust me."

Everyone around the table laughed, except for Alex.

Alex held my hand as we left the table, but he dropped it as soon as we were alone again. Neither of us spoke until we were both inside his car with the doors sealed shut.

"Holy shit," I said. "I did not see that wedding thing coming.

Although I guess I should have. Igor's right about spousal privilege."

Alex glared at me.

"What? We're not actually getting married." I stared at him. "You know that, right?"

"Oh no? I was ordered to buy you a ring. Ekatarina's meeting me at the jewelry store at three."

"Well, I hope her taste in jewelry is better than her taste in furnishings. Nothing gaudy, okay?"

Alex glared at me again.

"Fine, buy the gaudiest ring in the store. I really don't care *since we're not getting married!*"

"And what do you plan to tell Igor?"

"Come up to Santa Veneta this weekend. We'll tell Igor we got married at my aunt's house. He'll never know the difference."

Chapter 36

Fooling Igor was easy. Fooling the kids was a lot harder. I had to remember to take both rings—a surprisingly tasteful two-carat princess cut diamond in a platinum setting with a matching band—when I left the house in the morning. I kept them hidden in my purse until I dropped the kids off at camp. I slipped them on when I reached the office, but I had to remember to take them off again before I picked up the kids at the end of the day. I'd forgotten once and Sofia noticed right away and peppered me with questions. I pretended the rings were costume jewelry I'd bought for myself and she didn't know any better. If MJ had been paying attention, he might have questioned it, but he was wearing his earbuds and hadn't even looked up from his phone.

Although even if MJ had noticed the rings, I'm not sure he would've been suspicious since Alex was rarely home anymore. On weeknights it was just the kids and I who ate dinner together. After dinner we'd play a game or watch TV until it was time for Sofia to take a bath and go to bed. At that point, MJ usually went to his own bedroom, and I spent the rest of the evening alone.

Occasionally, Alex came home when I was still awake. On those nights we'd chat for a few minutes, then he'd go to his bedroom and I'd go to mine. Most nights he didn't come home until after I'd gone to bed. And sometimes he didn't come home at all.

I never asked him where he'd been or what he'd been doing, and he never offered an explanation. For all I knew, he was sleeping with another woman at his house in Boyle Heights. But that thought didn't make me jealous. Our physical relationship had ended the night he slammed me into a wall. Our interactions since then were tinged with an undercurrent of fear. I was afraid of what Alex might do if he got really angry at me again.

I was eager for the summer to end. I despised working for Igor even more now that he'd given me additional responsibility. In my old role I'd spent my days sitting in my windowless office drafting documents. When I moved assets for Igor, I did so electronically. But now that I was more deeply involved in his business, I took a more active role. These days I routinely left the office for in-person meetings and all my transactions were handled with cash.

I was the one who paid Igor's criminal defense attorneys, the ones who represented his men, and it was always men, when they got arrested. I also purchased and sold multiple properties for Igor's fake businesses. But the worst part of my job was when I had to pay people for their cooperation, whether those people wanted to cooperate or not. I often begged them to take the money, knowing if I couldn't persuade them, then one of Igor's henchmen would.

I always tried to schedule the "cooperation" visits for the end of the day. Afterwards I would pick up the kids from camp and drive us straight home, where I would immediately jump in the shower. Not that showering helped. Washing away my guilt wasn't that easy. I tried to console myself with the thought that as reprehensible as my actions were, they were in service to the larger goal of putting Igor behind bars for the rest of his life. If Igor was in prison, the lives of the people I threatened on his behalf would improve. Plus, if it hadn't been me, it would've been someone else on Igor's payroll, and likely someone a lot more willing to use violence to get what they wanted. While all of that was true, none of it made me feel any better.

I met with Agent Diaz once a week and dutifully reported all my actions. He always had lots of questions for me, but I only ever had one question for him: Did he have enough evidence to finally arrest Igor?

"If you were the one testifying against him, I'd have more than enough," Agent Diaz said. We were meeting at a park on this warm and sunny Saturday morning. Weekday meetings in LA were too difficult now that my duties for Igor had increased. Since I now carried large sums of cash, Igor insisted one of his men accompany me whenever I left the office. And I couldn't meet late at night or early in the morning anymore because of the kids. So Agent Diaz and I met on Saturday mornings after I dropped the kids off for their visit with Maria.

"Testifying is Alex's job, not mine. That was the deal." I took a sip of my to-go coffee while I watched other people's children play on the jungle gym.

Agent Diaz took a long swallow of his own to-go coffee. "Alex can only testify to conversations he participates in or overhears. Otherwise, it's hearsay."

I knew the law too, but that didn't make it any less frustrating. Even if I wore a wire, it wouldn't help because if the government introduced my recordings as evidence at trial, it would implicate me. Then I'd never be safe. That's why the plan had always been for Alex to testify against Igor. Then I could claim that Alex had duped me too. As long as I didn't offer any evidence against Igor, or more accurately, as long as the evidence I turned over to the FBI couldn't be traced back to me, I'd be safe.

"Then what do I do?" I asked. "School starts in two weeks. We need to wrap this up."

"Just because the kids are going back to Santa Veneta doesn't mean you have to. You could stay in LA and keep working for Igor. We'll get what we need eventually."

"No. I can barely stand living in my own skin anymore. The lying, the intimidation, the violence. I don't know how these people sleep at night." I was having a hard time myself, and I was just pretending to be a criminal.

Agent Diaz nodded. "It can be rough on agents. Undercover work isn't for everyone."

I thought about what Jake told me the night we'd had dinner. If it was just the lying that bothered me, I'd have gotten off easy. "I wasn't referring to your agents. I meant the criminals. Igor and Sergey and the rest of them."

"And Alex?" he asked.

I stared down at my coffee cup. I'd never told Agent Diaz about the night Alex pushed me into a wall. Sometimes I wondered if I wasn't partially to blame. Had I provoked him? He had told me not to do anything and I'd ignored him. Then I realized that's what battered women always say to excuse the behavior of their abusers. But there was no excuse for Alex's behavior that night. He was a violent man. That was the truth.

And yet, I didn't hate Alex or even dislike him, despite his violent tendencies and the fact he was a drug dealer. What bothered me about him most was he seemed to have no remorse about his career choice. I doubted Alex ever would've agreed to testify against Igor were it not for my involvement in this investigation. He would've kept on working for Igor and kept on providing the FBI just enough information to keep himself out of jail, until someone or something stopped him.

If that was all I knew about Alex, it would be easy to hate him, but the truth was more complicated. He had a tenderness to him I'd experienced firsthand and I was in awe of the sacrifice he was willing to make for his niece and nephew. Alex had agreed to go into Witness Protection, to uproot his life and never see his friends or family again, just so MJ and Sofia could keep living with me. I was having a hard time reconciling both sides of his personality.

When I didn't respond, Agent Diaz asked, "How are you two doing?"

"What do you mean?" I'd never told Agent Diaz Alex and I had slept together and I assumed Alex hadn't either.

"Living together," he said. "That's not always easy."

"It's fine. I barely see him."

Agent Diaz tossed his empty coffee cup into the trash as if he was shooting a basket—nothing but net—and turned back to me. "You live in the same house. How can you not see each other?"

"He's not home much these days. I think my fake husband might be cheating on me," I said and let out a laugh.

Agent Diaz laughed too. "I doubt that."

"Why? I have no hold on him. He can sleep with whoever he wants."

Agent Diaz's eyebrows raised and a smile played around his lips. "You two didn't hook up, did you?"

Not volunteering the information was one thing. Outright lying when asked was another. And what did it matter anymore? I hung my head and sighed. "He caught me in a weak moment."

Agent Diaz patted my shoulder. "Don't beat yourself up. You two would not be the first undercovers to cross that line."

"Really?" That surprised me.

"It happens more often than people like to admit. It's not

surprising really. You spend all your time with someone pretending to have feelings for them, then one day you wake up and realize you actually do have feelings for them or, at least, you do in that moment."

I was about to ask him if he had ever crossed that line with someone when he'd worked undercover when he jumped up. "I need to go. I promised my kid I'd be there for his soccer game this afternoon."

"Sure." I stood up too. "Do you have any advice for me to speed things up?"

"Just keep doing what you're doing."

"But what I'm doing isn't working, at least, not in the way we need it to."

"Be patient." Agent Diaz said. He walked a few paces away from me, stopped and turned around. "But if you happen to run across any incriminating documents—it's hard to refute a paper trail. But don't try to take them. Just snap pictures with your phone and send them to me." Then he spun back around and headed to the parking lot.

Chapter 37

AFTER MY MEETING with Agent Diaz, I drove to my house in Santa Veneta. I was surprised to see Alex's car parked in the driveway. He didn't tell me he was coming up this weekend. Although it had been a few days since we'd spoken.

I unlocked my front door and called out to him.

Alex appeared at the top of the stairs. "How was your meeting with Roberto?"

"How did you—"

"I saw him last night. He told me you two were meeting this morning."

"It was fine," I said. "What are you doing here? Why aren't you in LA?"

"I crashed here last night," he said as he jogged down the stairs. "I didn't think you'd mind. I promised Maria I'd help her put together a bunk bed today."

"A bunk bed? Please tell me she's not planning on having MJ and Sofia sleep in the same room again. He's sixteen."

"I think the plan is for her and Sofia to share the bedroom and MJ to sleep on the couch in the living room. But who knows if she'll even get custody again."

"She will." Janelle had told me as much. Maria had a job and an apartment and all her drug tests were clean. There was no reason for the judge to refuse her custody petition. I wasn't happy about it, but I was resigned.

Alex pulled his car keys out of his jeans pocket. "What are you up to tonight?"

"I'm supposed to be dropping off MJ at the movie theater around seven. Other than that, I'll be home with Sofia. I imagine we'll be watching something with a princess in it. You're welcome to join us if you'd like." I knew Sofia was disappointed she hadn't spent more time with Alex this summer.

"Hard pass on the princess movie but I need to talk to you. Is your mom still staying at your aunt's house?"

"Yes, until I move back. But I could probably get her to babysit for a couple of hours if I asked. If she complains, I'll just tell her I'm going on a date. Then she'll be shoving me out the front door."

Alex cracked a smile. "Where do you want to meet?"

"That depends. Are you going to take a swing at me again?"

"I didn't—" Alex stopped himself. "I would never hit you, Grace."

"You slammed my head into a wall."

"It was an accident. I just didn't want you to leave."

"And what would you have done if I'd stayed?"

He didn't answer me.

After a while I said, "I'd rather not have to worry about other people overhearing our conversation, so let's just meet back here. I promise to be on best behavior if you will."

He nodded.

"Okay. I'll text you when Sofia goes to bed."

. . .

Of course, tonight had to be one of those nights when Sofia refused to go to sleep. By the time I texted Alex, it was after ten and I was falling asleep myself.

Do you want to meet in the morning instead? I texted.

He texted back immediately: *Can't. Driving back tonight.*

So I pulled on my sweatshirt and sneakers and drove to my house.

If I didn't know it was my own house, I would've thought I was in the wrong place. The lights in the living room were dim, there was soft music playing, and a bottle of wine and two glasses sat out on the coffee table. I called out to Alex, who strolled out of my kitchen with a plate of cheese and crackers in his hand.

"What's all this?" I asked.

"I would've cooked," he said, "but I figured you'd already eaten."

"I'm not talking about the food. I thought you needed to talk to me. I didn't know this was a date." If I had, I wouldn't have come.

"It's not," he said. "I wanted to say goodbye."

"Goodbye?"

"I'm going into Witness Protection, Grace. You know what that means."

"But we still have two more weeks."

"I know, but I won't be around much. And I have a favor to ask. Please. It's important."

Chapter 38

We sat down on opposite ends of the couch and Alex poured us each a glass of red wine. Then he handed me a stack of paper that had been sitting on the coffee table.

"What is this?" I asked, although I recognized the legal forms.

"It's the paperwork for my house in LA. I want MJ and Sofia to have it. Can you help me with that?"

"I'm not an estate planning lawyer, Alex. I don't know all the ins and outs of transferring real property. But my guess is you can't transfer title to a minor, at least, not directly. You will likely need to set up a trust and appoint a trustee to oversee the property until they come of age. I can do some research for you if you'd like."

"Sounds complicated," he said. "Would it be easier if I gave the house to an adult?"

"Yes, I would think so."

"Then I'll transfer it to you."

"Me? Why me? Isn't there someone else?"

"Who? Maria? You think I would trust her with this?"

I understood. I wouldn't trust Maria either. "Okay. Transfer it to me and I'll figure out a way to transfer it to the kids."

"Thanks," he said and took a gulp of his wine.

I slid the paperwork under my purse so I wouldn't forget it. "Was that it?"

"No. Tell me how you plan on quitting your job with Igor. You know you can't just give two weeks' notice. That's not how this works."

I sighed and leaned my head back on the couch. I'd been worrying about this too. "I'm not sure. Every time I ask Agent Diaz, he brushes me off. I figured he had a plan, and he just hadn't shared it with me yet."

"His plan is for you to stay until he can arrest Igor."

"I told him I was leaving at the end of the summer. Multiple times."

Alex gulped down more wine and smacked his lips. "I know. He just doesn't believe you. He doesn't know you as well as I do."

I laughed. "Well, if he thinks he can get me to change my mind about this then that's definitely true."

Alex cracked a smile and offered me the plate of hors d'oeuvres. I took a square of cheddar and a handful of crackers, and we munched together in companionable silence.

"By the way," I said, "he knows we slept together."

"How?" Alex didn't seem upset by the news, just curious.

"He asked me directly and I couldn't lie."

"*Couldn't* lie?"

"Didn't lie. I'm tired of lying all the time. I just want to be a normal person again who generally tells the truth."

He nodded. "I know. I want that for you too. And for MJ and Sofia."

"I have no idea what I'm going to do with all my free time when they move back in with Maria. I spend half my evening trying to teach Sofia to read and the other half trying to get MJ to put down his phone."

Alex chuckled and shook his head. "That kid. I should take his phone away before I go."

"Don't bother. You know I'll just buy him another."

"You're too soft on him."

"No, you're too hard on him." I set down my wineglass and turned to face Alex. "Why have you been on his back all summer? He's a good kid. They're all addicted to their phones. We are too if you haven't noticed." I nodded to our respective cell phones, which were sitting on the coffee table. "We don't exactly set a good example."

Alex shrugged. "I suppose."

"And before I forget, next time you see Maria, tell her there's a meeting at Sofia's school first week in September that she needs to go to." The school sent the notice to my aunt because she's Sofia's current legal guardian. But if Maria regains custody, attending school meetings will be her responsibility.

"A meeting about what?" he asked.

"The results of the testing I forced them to do. I'm sure Sofia has dyslexia." For months I'd been trying to figure out why she wasn't learning to read. I knew she was intelligent, and she definitely tried. But it seemed like whatever progress she made with me at night, she'd forget it all the next day. Then I ran across an article on dyslexia and realized she had all the signs.

"Tell Maria the school's not going to want to provide the services Sofia needs because they're expensive. She's going to have to fight for them. Tell her if she's not comfortable going alone, I'd be happy to go with her, but somebody has to be there to advocate for Sofia."

Alex stared at me, a bemused expression on his face.

"What? You don't think we should hold the school accountable? Sofia is entitled to a free and appropriate public education just like every other child in this country. That's the law. And if the school principal hates me for forcing her to actually follow the law, then so be it. I don't really care what she thinks of me."

Alex grinned. "I wish I knew you when I was a kid, or someone like you."

"Why?"

He shook his head as if he was sorry he'd said anything. Then he refilled his wine glass and topped off mine. "We need to figure out how to get you away from Igor."

Neither of us had any ideas other than the obvious one—gathering enough evidence against Igor so that the FBI would arrest him. When both of us started yawning, I suggested we go to bed. I was too tired to drive home, and since Alex had drunk most of the wine, I didn't want him driving tonight either.

Alex's eyebrows shot up. "Are you inviting me upstairs?"

"No, I'm inviting you to spend the night on my couch."

I retrieved a set of sheets and a pillow and blanket from the linen closet, handed them to Alex, and said goodnight.

When I came downstairs the next morning, the bedding was folded and stacked on the corner of the couch and Alex was gone.

"Where were you all night?" my mother asked when I walked into my aunt's kitchen. I'd changed clothes, but my mother must've checked my room this morning. My aunt and Sofia were sitting at the table eating cereal and my mom was standing at the counter watching her bagel toast.

"I ended up sleeping at my house last night."

My mother's eyebrows raised and I knew she wanted to ask more questions, but she wouldn't in front of Sofia. When the toaster dinged, she pulled out her bagel and sat down at the table. I placed my own bagel in the toaster oven and popped a coffee pod into the Keurig machine. "Where's MJ?" I asked.

"Still sleeping," my mother said.

"MJ ate a whole pizza by himself yesterday," Sofia said. "Uncle Alex helped us build a bunk bed and took us out to lunch."

My mother shot me a pointed look. "I didn't know your uncle was in town this weekend. Grace, did you know?"

I didn't answer. Instead, I pulled my not quite toasted bagel out of the toaster oven and took a huge bite.

After breakfast I went upstairs to shower. I was still blow drying my hair when my mom knocked on my bedroom door. Before I could respond, she stepped inside and shut the door behind her. "Did you spend last night with Alex? Is that why you asked me to babysit?"

"Yes, but it's not what you think. He slept on the couch."

"I don't understand this relationship."

"Because it's not a relationship. It's a work thing. And soon you're not going to have to worry about it because he's leaving."

"Where's he going?"

"I'm not sure," I said, realizing that was true, "but he won't be living in California anymore." I had no idea where the Marshal's service would relocate Alex, but I was sure they would move him to another state.

"You do realize someday you're going to have to explain all this to me."

I shrugged and my mother let out an exasperated sigh. I understood. I was exasperated with the situation too.

"Okay, Gracie, but I'm supposed to be going home in two weeks. Can you at least tell me if you'll be back by then?"

"Yes, I promise."

. . .

ALEX and I met with Agent Diaz the following week. It was the first time the three of us had sat down together in over a month. I needed to ditch Igor's men, so I told Igor I had a gynecologist appointment that could take several hours. I knew the word "gynecologist" would do the trick. As an added precaution, I drove to the medical offices attached to the big hospital in Beverly Hills and left my car in the patient parking lot. Then I used the building's internal walkway to access the hospital, where Alex was waiting for me in the underground garage.

Instead of meeting Agent Diaz in a parking lot in LA, we drove out to a truck stop in the desert. Agent Diaz was waiting for us at a picnic table in the shade. It was brutally hot in the desert this time of year, and I started sweating the moment I left Alex's air-conditioned car. Agent Diaz handed us each a bottle of cold water and I downed half of mine in one gulp. My sleeveless silk shirt was already sticking to my chest and back.

Alex was the one who pressed Agent Diaz on an exit strategy for me.

"The plan hasn't changed," Agent Diaz told him. "You two get me the evidence I need to arrest Igor, then you testify against him at trial, and Igor spends the rest of his life in federal prison. You get a new identity courtesy of Witsec, Grace can go back to her life in Santa Veneta and, hopefully, I get a promotion so I can get the hell out of LA."

"Except I'm leaving in ten days," I said, "and we still don't have enough evidence."

Agent Diaz sighed. "Grace, you don't just resign from an organized crime family. They call it a family for a reason. Surely, you've seen *a Godfather* movie or an episode of *The Sopranos*."

"You told me this wasn't like the movies!"

"It's not. But that doesn't mean some stereotypes don't hold true."

I turned to Alex, who said, "Igor thinks we're married. Once I turn on him, won't he assume Grace will too?"

Agent Diaz pointed his water bottle at Alex. "I've been thinking about that. We need to put some daylight between you two. Let Igor believe there's trouble in paradise. Grace already thinks you have a mistress. She should let it slip to Igor, maybe wonder aloud what else you're keeping from her."

Alex turned to me. "You think I have a mistress?"

"You're never home at night," I said. "What am I supposed to think?"

"Don't overplay it," Agent Diaz admonished me. "We don't want Igor getting suspicious."

Alex nodded at Agent Diaz. "He knows where I am at night, and it's not with another woman."

"Loose lips sink ships," Agent Diaz said then turned back to me. "The way I see it, you have three choices." He held up his thumb. "You stay as long as it takes to get the evidence we need."

"No," I said. "You've only got me for ten more days."

Agent Diaz raised his index finger. "You can testify against Igor and we'll put you in Witness Protection too."

I shook my head. "No way."

Agent Diaz threw up his whole hand. "Then find me something I can use against Igor that doesn't involve your participation in a trial."

Chapter 39

I STARED out the car window at the barren hills punctuated by the occasional strip mall as Alex drove us back towards LA. "I need to search those file cabinets."

"No," Alex said.

"What do you mean, no? You heard him. We need evidence that doesn't require my testimony. That's lawyer-speak for documents."

"Then let me look for them."

"Oh yeah, that won't be suspicious. When have you ever combed through Igor's files? It's what I do, Alex. I'm his lawyer."

Alex spied the cop's car up ahead and slowed down to the speed limit. "Not the ones in the file cabinets. They're locked."

"I found the key."

"When?"

"A while ago." I didn't tell Alex I'd already snooped once because I knew he'd get angry.

Alex's jaw clenched and he shook his head. "Grace, you need to listen to me. I will find a way to get Roberto what he needs. I do not want you taking unnecessary risks."

"Fine," I said. "No unnecessary risks." Alex and I just had different definitions of the word "unnecessary."

I COULDN'T GO to the gallery over the weekend because Igor knew I took the kids to Santa Veneta every weekend to see their mother. But snooping on a weekday was dangerous because I never knew when Igor or one of his men might show up. I needed a time when no one else would be there and the only time I could think of was a Thursday night.

I'd finally gotten Alex to tell me why Igor cancelling plans on a Thursday night was such a big deal. Every Thursday night Igor's wife Ekaterina went out with her girlfriends, all young Russian women who'd married older rich men too. On Thursday nights Igor's crew gathered at his house for a night of debauchery. I'd asked Alex if that meant prostitutes too or if it was only drugs and alcohol. He pled the fifth.

Since Alex told me he always went to these parties, I assumed he'd be there this Thursday night too. I was shocked when he walked into the house while the kids and I were eating dinner.

"What are you doing here?" I asked, as he sat down next to MJ at the kitchen table.

"I live here, remember," Alex said.

Sofia giggled. She was obviously happy to have Alex home since she was grinning ear to ear. MJ was just as obviously not happy to have Alex home. He stared down at his plate and stabbed at his lasagna with his fork.

"Isn't there somewhere you're supposed to be tonight?" I said and gave Alex a meaningful look.

"I cancelled," he said and sniffed at the lasagna pan sitting in the center of the table. "Smells good. Can I have some?"

I couldn't take credit for the meal since I'd picked it up at the grocery store on the way home. All I'd had to do was heat it up. "Sure. Plates are in the cabinet and silverware is in the drawer."

MJ snickered and Alex shot him a warning glance. But he did retrieve his own plate and utensils, along with a beer. And I served him a slice of lasagna.

I waited until the kids finished eating and left the table before I brought up Igor again. "I think you should go to the party. We don't want Igor getting suspicious."

"He's not," Alex said. "And I'm tired."

He looked tired. He had the same dark circles under his eyes I had under mine, except I covered mine with makeup. The stress was taking a toll on both of us.

Alex swigged the rest of his beer and set the bottle down on the table. "I just want to stay home and watch the game tonight, if that's alright with you."

"Fine," I said. "I won't be here anyway. I'm meeting my brother-in-law for a drink." It was the first lie that popped into my head. "I'll probably be home late."

"You can come home whenever you want. You don't have a curfew."

"I know. I just didn't want you to worry."

Alex stared at me. "Why would I worry?"

"No reason."

I stood up to clear the dishes. When I reached across the table for Alex's plate, he grabbed my wrist. "Are you lying to me?"

"No," I said, pulling my hand away. "Why would I lie?"

I'd become such an accomplished liar these past few months that he believed me.

. . .

The gallery was dark when I arrived, but the motion sensor lights turned on as I approached the front door. I wasn't concerned since I knew they'd turn off again once I was inside. I unlocked the door, shut off the alarm, and headed to my office. For once I was grateful there were no windows. It meant I could turn on all the lights and no one outside the building would be able to see.

I dumped out the container of paperclips onto my desk and plucked the key ring from the pile. Then I unlocked the first file cabinet and got to work.

Hours later I'd still found nothing, or at least nothing that was going to put Igor in prison for the rest of his life. I'd spread out the contents of the first two file cabinets on the rug because there was way too much paper for me to sort through it all on my desk. I'd organized the documents into piles. There were invoices, bills of sale, receipts for everything from artwork to toilet paper, tax returns, and ledgers, which might or might not be useful depending on whether they were accurate. But there was nothing that jumped out at me as a smoking gun. I finally decided to just start photographing everything. I'd send it all to Agent Diaz and let him sort it out. The FBI probably employed an army of forensic accountants whose job it was to comb through financial documents.

It was almost midnight when I stood up to stretch and get myself more coffee. After a bathroom break, I returned to the office and knelt down on the rug again. I finished sorting the pile I'd been working on and as I spun around to grab another stack of paper, I accidentally knocked over my coffee cup.

"Fuck!" The brown liquid was spreading everywhere.

I ran back to the kitchen, grabbed the roll of paper towels, and hurried back to my office. The documents were my priority so I saved them first. Some of the ink had blurred on a few of the pages, but the vast majority of them were still readable even through the coffee stains. When I'd sopped up all the liquid, I went back to the kitchen for a sponge and dish soap. I didn't know if the oriental rug was valuable or just a cheap knock off, but either way I needed to get rid of the giant coffee stain because I didn't want to have to explain how it got there.

I moved the piles of documents to the couch then I got down on my hands and knees and started scrubbing. I was working on a particularly stubborn spot when I first felt it. I'd been kneeling on this rug for hours. The cement floor underneath was hard and flat, yet this section had an indentation.

I sat back on my butt and ran my hand over the spot. All I felt was damp wool. But when I got back up onto my knees again, I felt something uneven underneath me. Either the cement floor under the rug was cracked, which was possible since this was earthquake country, or there was something underneath.

I tried rolling up the rug from the side closest to the couch, but I couldn't get it back far enough to reach the uneven spot. The only way to get to it would be to move my desk. I closed my eyes and sighed. It was late, I was tired, and it was probably nothing anyway, but I'd come too far to quit now.

After a fair amount of swearing, I was eventually able to move the heavy desk far enough back that I could roll up the rug.

"Holy shit!"

I reached for my phone. Agent Diaz definitely needed to see this.

Chapter 40

SOMEONE HAD CUT a hole in the cement floor and installed a two foot by two foot wooden door. Whoever had built it had done a good job. But for a thin metal strip around the edge of the frame, which only raised it by millimeters, it was flush with the cement. My knee must've landed on the handle, which was inlaid metal but with a small groove to lift up the ring.

As soon as I opened the trap door the light inside the small basement turned on. I climbed down the ladder and stared open-mouthed at the huge pile of money. I'd never seen this much cash before. There had to be millions of dollars. Or more likely tens of millions of dollars. It was how I imagined banks stacked money in their vaults, except this cash was sitting on a wood pallet like boxes of cereal at Costco.

The room wasn't wide, but it was deep. The pallet of cash was at the far end. The adjacent walls were lined with long black duffel bags. I unzipped the one closest to me, thinking it was probably filled with brick-sized packages of white powder like you see on the news when there's a drug bust. But the duffel bags were filled with long guns. The kinds of guns people use to kill other people, not deer.

"Holy shit," I said again and pulled my phone out of my back pocket. I snapped pictures of the money and the guns, but the light in the basement was dim, and the photos came out dark and grainy. I was fumbling with the flash button when I heard voices above me.

Chapter 41

I GLANCED around the basement but there was nowhere to hide. Then I looked up and saw Sergey staring down at me. He was kneeling on the cement floor above my head. "Get out," he said in his heavily accented English.

I froze. I knew I needed to come up with an excuse why I was there, but my mind was blank.

"Now," Sergey shouted.

My heart was pounding so fast and so loud he must've heard it too. I couldn't move. I couldn't think. All I could do was mutely stare up at him.

Then he pointed a gun at my forehead. "Move or I shoot you right there."

The gun broke me out of my stupor. I was still terrified, but I could at least get my limbs to move. I stuffed my phone into my back pocket and started climbing the ladder. Not fast enough for Sergey though, because after two rungs, he reached down and grabbed me under the arm and pulled me up the rest of the way. When my head cleared the trap door, I saw that Igor was in the office too. He was standing with his back to me staring at the stacks of paper on the couch.

Once my feet hit the floor, Sergey grabbed me by my hair and pushed me forward. I yelped. That's when Igor turned around. He was glassy-eyed, I assumed from drugs or alcohol or both, but he looked sad too. He swept my meticulously organized piles of paper onto the floor and sat down heavily on the couch.

"It's not what you think," I said.

Igor held one meaty finger to his lips and shushed me. "Don't lie." His Russian accent was thicker than usual. "It won't help you."

"Where should I take her?" Sergey asked as he tightened his already tight grip on the back of my head.

"Don't be in such a hurry," Igor said. "Let's find out what she knows first."

"I don't know anything," I cried.

Igor gave me a disappointed look. "What did I just say? No lying."

"I'm not lying," I cried again.

Sergey jerked my head back, so I was staring up at him. He flicked open a switchblade and pushed the tip of the knife into the side of my neck. "You lie again I slit your throat and watch you bleed." Then he pushed my head forward, so I was facing Igor again.

Igor shook his head. "Watching someone bleed to death is not an easy thing. I'd rather put a bullet in your head. Less painful for both of us."

That's when I felt the wet warmth spreading through my underwear and trickling down my leg. *Please, please, please. I don't want to die.*

"Where's Alex?" he asked.

I tried to shake my head, but I couldn't. Sergey's grip was too tight. "I don't know." My mind leapt to the kids. If I told him Alex was at the house, they might go there and kill the kids too.

"Don't lie to me," Igor shouted and Sergey yanked my hair again.

"I'm not lying!" I screamed, my survival instinct finally kicking in. "Most nights he doesn't come home. I never know where he is."

"You leave your children home alone?" Igor asked.

"MJ's sixteen," I said. "He's old enough to babysit."

Igor's anger dissipated and the sadness returned. "I pay you well, no? You ask for more responsibility, I give to you. I'm good boss."

"You are," I stammered. "I wasn't stealing from you if that's what you think."

"Then what were you doing with my money?" Igor demanded.

"Nothing. I swear. I had no idea that room even existed until tonight."

Igor leaned back on the couch and folded his arms across his chest. I felt like minutes passed, but it could've been seconds. "I believe you," Igor finally said, nodding. "You know why I believe you? Because that room has camera. It turns on when you open the door."

That must be why he and Sergey came to the gallery in the middle of the night. I must've triggered some sort of silent alarm. God, I was such an idiot.

"Why were you taking pictures?" Igor asked.

"To send to Alex. I didn't think he'd believe me if I told him there was a secret room under my desk."

Igor laughed. "You think Alex doesn't know? Who do you think put the guns there?"

It was as if he'd punched me. My whole body slumped. I probably would've fallen to my knees if Sergey wasn't holding me up by my hair. *Alex knew about this room the whole time and didn't tell me? Did Agent Diaz know too? Were they both working for Igor? Was I wrong about everything?*

"Either you're very good actress or I think you really didn't know," Igor said.

"I didn't know," I said, defeated.

Igor nodded. "Call your husband. Let's see what he has to say."

"What?" When I heard the word *husband,* I still immediately thought of Jonah.

"Call Alex. Tell him he needs to come to the gallery right away. No funny business or we shoot you and he finds your body."

My hands were shaking so badly that when I pulled my phone out of my pocket, I dropped it on the floor. But I couldn't reach down to pick it up because Sergey was still holding me by my hair. I shifted my eyes to the ground then back up at Igor.

"Dope," he said to Sergey, "get her phone."

Sergey pushed me down to the floor. Hard. I snatched up my phone and he pulled me upright again by my hair. The pain in the back of my head was intense, but it was keeping me alert.

I held the phone up to my face and the screen unlocked. My hands were still shaking, but I managed to tap on the icons without dropping it again. Alex's number was saved in my favorites. After a momentary delay the call went through. The phone rang once on my end. A second later we all heard the corresponding ring in the gallery.

Chapter 42

It happened so fast it was a blur. Alex appeared in the doorway with a gun in his hand. Then shouting in Russian, an explosion, and he disappeared again. I smelled smoke and tried to run, but Sergey was still holding me by my hair. He was dragging me toward the trap door.

"Alex!" I screamed.

He appeared in the doorway again, but this time he was pointing his gun at me, or more likely at Sergey, who was standing behind me, using me as a human shield. Sergey still had one hand wrapped in my hair. His other hand was holding a gun but this time it was pointed at Alex.

I slid my eyes to the couch. Igor was lying down in an awkward position, his head covered in blood. His eyes were open, and he was staring at me. I didn't want to look at him, but I was transfixed. It wasn't until I heard Alex shouting my name that I glanced away.

"Are you hurt?" Alex asked.

I was too terrified to speak. I just stared at him.

"Give her to me," Alex said to Sergey.

"No," Sergey replied and jerked my head back again.

"Igor's dead. There's no reason for you to kill her."

"She knows me," he said.

"She's my wife. She's not gonna talk."

Sergey pulled me closer. "I'll kill you too."

"Sergey, think," Alex said. "With Igor gone, we could take over. Run it together. Just you and me."

"I don't need partner," Sergey said.

"Okay," Alex said. "Then we'll split it. Take half and leave, but Grace stays with me."

"How do I know you won't kill me too?" Sergey said as he inched us closer to the trap door.

"Why would I kill you?" Alex said as he moved deeper into the office. "There's enough for both of us. But you're not leaving here with my wife."

"I need insurance policy," Sergey said.

We all heard the sirens and instinctively turned in their direction. But this was LA. The sound of sirens was not uncommon. Police, fire, ambulance—there was no way to know which one it was or if it was coming here.

"We're running out of time," Alex said.

"Okay," Sergey said. "You wait here." Then he pushed me through the trapdoor and jumped in after me.

I landed on my shoulder and pain shot through my arm, but my head hurt slightly less. I looked up and saw Sergey pull the trapdoor shut and bolt it. I started to push myself up when Sergey pointed his gun at me. "Stay down and don't move."

I stayed on the ground and silently watched as he grabbed the two closest duffel bags. He dumped the guns out of one of them and rushed to the pallet of money. He stuffed handfuls of cash inside until it was full. He zipped it shut and slung it over his shoulder, and grabbed the duffel with the guns and slung it over his other shoulder. Then he pulled his handgun out of his waistband and pointed it at me. "Stand up."

I scrambled to my feet.

Sergey unbolted the trapdoor and popped it open. "We're coming out," he shouted. "You shoot me, I shoot her. *Da*?"

"Yes," Alex shouted back. "And if you kill her, it'll be the last thing you ever do."

Sergey didn't answer him. He just pushed me into the ladder and said, "Go."

I climbed the rungs with his gun in my back.

"Stop," he said, when I still had two rungs left. Then he grabbed me around the waist and launched both of us onto the cement floor. I think we were meant to land on our butts with me on top of him, but one of the duffel bags caught on the corner of the trap door and we both fell onto our sides.

Sergey still had his arm around my waist, and I was trying to wriggle free, when I looked up and saw Alex's gun. Then I heard the explosion.

Chapter 43

ALL I COULD HEAR WAS RINGING in my ears, but I could see Sergey's face, or what was left of it. Blood and brains were splattered everywhere, and the smell of smoke was overpowering. I vomited all over the floor and started shivering uncontrollably. I heard Alex's voice in the distance, as if it was coming from the end of a long tunnel. He grabbed me by the shoulders and shook me, then he lifted me onto my feet.

I stared up into his familiar face.

"You need to leave." My purse appeared out of nowhere and he pushed my car keys into my hand. "Go home, get the kids, and take them to your house. Not your aunt's house. Your house. Do you understand?"

When I didn't respond, he shook me again and repeated his instructions. "Grace, answer me."

This time I nodded mutely.

He searched the ground for my phone and dropped it into my purse. "I will call you when it's safe. Now go."

I nodded again but I didn't move.

He put his warm hands on both sides of my face and forced me to look at him. "Grace, you have to go now. Please."

. . .

I DON'T KNOW if it was his calm voice in the midst of the chaos or the sirens blaring outside or the overwhelming smell of smoke in the air, but something propelled me to move. I walked out of the gallery, got into my car, and drove home. According to the clock on my dashboard it was 2:36 am. I pulled out onto the street, which was dark and empty, or as empty as the streets ever were in LA.

Ten minutes later I pulled into the driveway of our house. My brain was working now, but slowly. I went to MJ's room first. I don't know why I didn't turn on the light, but I didn't. I shook him awake.

"We need to leave," I said.

"What?" he answered sleepily.

"Now," I shouted. "We need to leave now."

He turned on the lamp next to his bed and stared up at me, horrified. I looked down and saw what he saw. One side of my white shirt was covered in blood.

"It's not mine," I said. "But we need to leave."

He nodded and kicked off his blanket.

I wiped at my face and realized I was crying, but I kept moving. I went to Sofia's room next. I pulled off her covers and tried to lift her out of bed, but I was having a hard time maneuvering her. MJ came in and handed me a T-shirt, one of his. He nodded at my chest. "You'll scare her."

I pulled my blood soaked shirt over my head and dropped it on the floor. I pulled his shirt on while he lifted Sofia out of her bed. Her eyes opened, but she wasn't fully awake. She stared up at both of us but didn't say a word.

"Should we pack?" he asked.

"No," I said, and he followed me outside.

We were speeding north on the freeway before I wondered if I'd remembered to lock the front door. I had no idea.

Sometime later MJ asked, "Where are we going?"

"Home," I said. "My home."

"Is Uncle Alex coming too?"

"I don't know."

It was still dark outside when we arrived at my house in Santa Veneta. I parked in the garage, which I never did, and sent the kids upstairs to my bedroom. I laid down on the living room couch with the phone next to my ear. But I was too keyed up to sleep. When the sky turned pink, I clicked on the television. I was hoping to see something on the news about what had happened, but the local Santa Veneta stations didn't cover the daily violence in LA. I shut off the TV and started googling on my phone. I couldn't find anything about a shooting at an art gallery.

When the kids came downstairs a couple of hours later, Alex still hadn't called.

"Do you have anything to eat?" MJ asked.

"Not much." The last time I was at my house was that night with Alex. We didn't finish all the cheese and crackers, but he may have thrown away what was left. I pulled my wallet out of my purse and handed MJ my credit card. "Order whatever you want for delivery."

"What should I get you?" MJ asked.

"Nothing," I said. "I'm not hungry."

When the food arrived, MJ handed me something warm wrapped in white butcher paper. "I got you a bagel. In case you change your mind."

I thanked him and left it on the coffee table. I wanted to call Alex, but I was afraid to. He'd told me he'd call me when it was safe. This time I was going to do what he told me to do.

When my phone finally rang an hour later, I jumped. The caller ID showed a blocked number, but I answered it anyway.

"Alex?"

"Roberto," he said. "Agent Diaz."

"Where's Alex?"

"I don't know. I was hoping you did."

Chapter 44

I ORDERED an Uber to take the kids to my aunt's house and gave them strict instructions not to tell my aunt or my mother anything.

"They're going to ask where you are," MJ said.

He and Sofia were still wearing their pajamas. That alone was going to elicit questions.

"Tell them I'm at my house and I'll come over later and explain everything. But for right now, tell them I need you all to stay there. I don't want any of you coming here."

MJ looked at me doubtfully, but said, "Okay. I'll try."

Agent Diaz arrived two hours later.

I heard his car pull into the driveway. I opened my front door as he was walking up the stone path. I was used to seeing him in a business suit, at least on weekdays, but today he was wearing khakis and a blue and gold FBI jacket. "Did you hear from Alex?" I asked.

He shook his head. "You?"

"No. He said he'd call me when it was safe. Maybe I should call him."

"Don't bother," Agent Diaz said. "He's already dumped his phone."

"How do you—"

"We were tracking him. You too."

"You were tracking me?" My voice cracked.

"As a precaution. It's standard procedure. Be thankful we did. That's how I knew where you were when you sent me that picture. I called Alex and told him he needed to get to the gallery pronto before you ruined everything."

"Before I ruined everything?" My voice was even higher now.

Agent Diaz glanced around my foyer. "Can we sit down? I need to get a statement from you."

My lawyer brain switched on at "statement." "Am I in trouble?"

"No. I just need to know everything that happened last night."

We sat at my kitchen table and I told Agent Diaz everything I could remember. Occasionally, he interrupted me with a question, but mostly he let me talk. I kept my phone on the table next to me the entire time, but it never rang.

When I finished, Agent Diaz closed the pad he'd been using to take notes.

"What should I do now?" I asked as he stood up.

"Whatever you want. The investigation's over. Everyone's dead."

"What do you mean, everyone?" I only knew about Igor and Sergey.

"We're still looking for Mischa. But his orange Lamborghini shouldn't be too hard to find. Everyone else in Igor's crew is dead."

"How? It was only Igor and Sergey at the gallery."

"I can't say for sure, but my suspicion is after Alex sent you away, he went to Igor's house and killed them. The guard at the gate and all three men inside were shot in the head at close range. That doesn't happen by accident."

"But why would Alex kill them? He had no reason."

"Because they knew you, Grace. He was trying to keep you, and by extension the kids, safe."

"But you would've just arrested them. Surely with the money and the guns, you have enough evidence now."

"Yes. We would've arrested everyone. But it looks like Alex had other ideas."

I sat at the table in stunned silence. I'd witnessed Alex shoot Igor and Sergey. But if he hadn't, they would've killed me and maybe him too. It was self-defense. But why go to Igor's house and kill everyone else? He could've just testified against them at trial, and they would've ended up in prison.

I shook my head and stared up at Agent Diaz. "I don't understand any of this."

He reached down and patted my shoulder. "Because you're not a criminal. It may not make sense to you, but it makes perfect sense to Alex."

"But he was going to testify. He was going to go into Witness Protection. We talked about it just a few days ago."

Agent Diaz pulled on his jacket. "Maybe if things had gone differently, he would have. Or maybe he felt like he had no choice. I don't know. But he's disappeared with millions of dollars and a couple dozen assault rifles."

"How do you—"

"Igor had a security camera in the basement. We found the feed."

My heart sunk. Maybe Alex felt like he needed the guns for protection. Although why would he need two dozen of them? But there was only one reason to take the money. "What happens to him now?"

"We put out an APB. But with that much cash, it shouldn't be too difficult for him to disappear. If he contacts you, please call me." I don't know why he placed his business card on the table. Obviously, I had his number.

After Agent Diaz left I called my aunt's house. My mother answered the phone.

"Where are you?" she demanded.

"My house. Didn't MJ tell you?"

"Yes, and that's all he would tell me. You send the kids over here unannounced, still in their pajamas—"

"Why do they have to be announced? They live their too."

That threw her off her tirade. "Yes, well, I don't like any of this. You either come over here right now and tell us what's going on, or we're coming to you."

I sighed. "Okay, Mom, give me an hour." I needed a shower and a cup of coffee. I hadn't slept and I was still wearing my peed-in jeans and MJ's sweat-stunk T-shirt.

Chapter 45

MJ ENTERTAINED Sofia so I could speak to my mom and my aunt alone. They were alternately furious with me and thankful I was safe. When I'd answered all their questions, I swore them both to secrecy. I didn't know if any of this was still confidential since the investigation was over, but I told them it was because I didn't want my mom blabbing about it to her entire fifty-five and over community. I assumed my aunt would be more circumspect, but my admonition left no doubt.

I pulled MJ outside to the patio and told him what I knew. He sat on the foot of the lounge chair with his head hung down and it reminded me of the day Jake had sat in that same spot and confessed his part in Jonah and Amelia's murder. Was this nightmare finally over? I hoped so.

"Do you think Uncle Alex will ever come back?" he asked.

"I don't know. The FBI doesn't seem to think so. If he does, he'll be in a lot of trouble."

"And he was just going to go into Witness Protection and never see us again?"

"That's how Witness Protection works, MJ. It's the only

way to keep people safe. He wanted you and Sofia to have a normal life."

MJ wiped his runny nose with the back of his hand and blinked back tears. "Yeah, sure. Like our life with our mother is so normal."

I reached out and squeezed his hand. "You still have me. Even if you're living with your mother, you know you can always call me. And we'll still see each other. I'm still coming to all your basketball games. You can't stop me. And I'm still going to make you dress up for dances and take embarrassing photos of you and talk to you about sex even though you don't want me to. You know that, right? You're stuck with me."

He nodded and the tears spilled out onto his cheeks.

I scooted over so our knees were touching, and we held each other's hand and cried until we both ran out of tears.

MJ and I talked to Sofia together. We tried to explain what happened while only giving her a sanitized version of events. She seemed more confused than anything, but when we told her we didn't know if or when she'd see Alex again, she cried too.

The next week passed in a blur. Agent Diaz asked me to come down to his office because he had more questions for me. And I needed to return to the house in LA to pack up our belongings.

I found my bloody shirt on the floor of Sofia's bedroom where I'd dropped it. I tossed it into the trash then packed up our things, mine first, then the kids'. I left Alex's bedroom for last. I stared at the black jeans and black shirts hanging in his closet. What was I supposed to do with them? It didn't feel right to throw them away, but why save them? Alex wasn't coming back. He knew if he did, he'd be arrested.

I checked my phone incessantly for a voicemail or a text, anything to let me know he was safe. But nothing ever came. I didn't even know if he was alive anymore. But I couldn't bring myself to throw away his clothes, so I folded everything and placed it all in the shopping bags I'd brought from home. I didn't think MJ would want any of it, but I'd give him the option.

After I cleaned out Alex's closet, I moved to his dresser. I smiled when I found the wallet. It was still in its box. Alex had never used it. But the money clip was gone.

Janelle called while I was driving home.

"Are you sitting down?" she asked.

"Yes, I'm stuck in traffic on the 101. I'll probably be here for hours. What's up?"

"I just got off the phone with the kids' social worker. Maria's back in jail."

"What! How the hell did that happen?"

"She got picked up last night. The paramedics Narcan'd her and took her to the hospital, and they called the cops. Her parole officer was already looking for her because she missed a drug test."

"How is this even possible? She's been clean for months. She had a job, an apartment. She was getting the kids back."

Janelle sighed. "Unfortunately, it's not that uncommon. She's lucky the paramedics found her when they did. Otherwise, we'd be planning her funeral."

I sighed too. "Jesus, Janelle. Do the kids know?"

"No, I wanted to tell you first. Can you bring them by my office tomorrow? I'd rather tell them in person than over the phone."

"Sure. What time? School doesn't start until next week so we're free all day."

"Come by in the morning around ten. Maybe you and I can talk separately first."

"About?" What other bad news did she have that was so awful she didn't want to tell me over the phone?

"Well, it's been over a year since your suicide attempt."

"And you're bringing that up now because?" I said testily.

"Because MJ and Sofia will need to stay in foster care longer than we anticipated. I was wondering if you wanted to apply."

I didn't answer because I was stunned.

"You'd have to meet with a psychiatrist who'd have to certify you're mentally stable," she continued. "Otherwise, it's just the usual routine. Submit to a home study, complete the training seminar, etcetera. You up for it?"

Chapter 46

"You HAVE the most exciting life of all my patients," Dr. Rubenstein said, and I laughed. This was the first time I'd seen her since my life blew up. Again.

"Happy to be of service. I'll be sure to let you know the next time I almost get myself murdered by Russian mobsters."

This time we both laughed.

"Seriously, Grace, how are you feeling?"

I shook my head and mock sighed. "It's always about the feelings with you."

She nodded sagely. "It is."

I took a deep breath and let it out slowly. "Honestly, I still can't wrap my head around what Alex did. I mean, I understand why he shot Igor and Sergey. He had no choice. But the rest of them—I'm not saying the world's not a better place without these men in it. But to execute them, especially when he didn't have to..."

"Maybe he thought he did have to. Maybe he thought these men would come after you and the kids and it was the only way to keep you all safe."

"But the FBI would've arrested them. They would've gone to prison."

Dr. Rubenstein shrugged. "I don't know, Grace. Only Alex can answer these questions. How are you feeling about applying to become a foster parent?"

"Excited. And scared. And a little sad too."

"Sad?"

"For Maria. She was doing so well. I don't understand why she started using again. And sad for the kids too. They feel abandoned by her. Again."

"Addiction is an illness, Grace."

"I know that. I'm just telling you how they feel."

"And have you given any thought to what's next for you, apart from the foster parenting?"

"Not really. I guess at some point I'll go back to work. Not that I have an office anymore. Or clients."

"You could always get a job at another law firm."

"Yeah, I suppose." That thought didn't excite me, but it wasn't as if I had a better idea.

"Are you going to continue to live with your aunt?"

I nodded. "I told my mom I'd stay, at least, until she's able to drive again. After that, I'm not sure. If I get approved as MJ and Sofia's foster parent, then maybe the three of us will move to my house."

"You've decided to keep your house? Because at one time you talked about selling it and moving somewhere new, somewhere with less memories."

"The memories don't bother me as much anymore. And if I live there with MJ and Sofia, we'll make new memories, won't we?"

When our time was up, we agreed to keep meeting once a week. I knew the day would come when I wouldn't see Dr.

Rubenstein anymore, but I felt like I wasn't ready to give her up yet. Someday, but not today.

I received the text from my OB/GYN's office asking me to confirm my appointment while I was in my session with Dr. Rubenstein. I'd completely forgotten about it. I was going to cancel the appointment since I no longer needed the birth control pills, then I realized the last time I'd seen my OB/GYN was when Amelia was alive. Since I was long overdue for a checkup, I texted back *yes* to confirm. Then I drove to my house to pick up my mail.

I was sitting at my kitchen table, sorting the junk from the bills, when I spotted the letter with the San Diego postmark and no return address. I probably would've thrown it away if I hadn't recognized Alex's handwriting. I tore open the envelope and pulled out the handwritten note. The paper looked like it was torn from a legal pad. It could've been one of mine.

Dear Grace,

I'm sure by now you know everything. And knowing you, I'm sure you have questions. I'll try to answer some.

I didn't tell you about the basement because I thought you'd never find it. I should've known better. You're probably upset about the guns too. You're not gonna want to hear this but those guns were for you. It was a way for me to get evidence on Igor so you could leave.

I'm sure you're not happy about the rest of it either. No one got anything they didn't deserve. But I can still hear your voice in my head. Why didn't you just let the FBI arrest them? Because those men knew you and I wanted to be sure you and the kids were safe. I protect the people I love. So do you. We just go about it in different ways.

And that's why I gave Maria the drugs. It was her choice to take them. But I knew she would. She's an addict. That's what addicts do. And after everything I'd done, I wasn't about to let

Maria fuck it all up. The kids are better off with you. We both know it.

There's one more thing I need to tell you. Or ask you. I think you call it a quid pro quo. Remember when you told me about the big life insurance policy your husband left you? I respected him for that. A man provides for his family. But I can't go buy a life insurance policy like your husband did. So I left something under your bathroom sink.

I know when you see it you'll want to call Roberto. Please don't. You wanted justice for your family and I gave it to you. Maybe not in the way you wanted, but be honest. Isn't there a part of you that's glad Igor and his crew are dead? Now you'll never have to think about them again.

So I'm asking for a quid pro quo. Give MJ and Sofia the life your parents gave you. The one my parents wanted to give me and Maria but couldn't.

Love,

Alex

I set down the letter and cried. Then I went upstairs and looked under my bathroom sink.

Chapter 47

I NEVER WOULD'VE FOUND the package Alex had left for me if he hadn't told me it was there. He'd installed a false panel in the bathroom cabinet under my sink. Behind it, sealed in plastic wrap that had probably come from my kitchen, were three tall stacks of cash. Almost one and a half million dollars I discovered after I counted it.

Alex was right. My first thought was to call Agent Diaz and turn everything over to the FBI. But I fought my instincts. My emotions were too raw right now to make this decision. I needed time to think. I carefully rewrapped the cash and returned it to its hiding place under the sink. Then I went back downstairs to the kitchen and ripped up Alex's letter into tiny pieces.

I was reeling from his confession about Maria. Maybe I should've realized she'd gotten the drugs from him, but it had honestly never occurred to me. I knew Alex wanted the kids to live with me, and I did too, but to sabotage his own sister? I would have to live with the knowledge it was Alex who gave Maria the drugs that sent her back to jail, but I would never tell MJ or Sofia. If Maria chose to tell them someday, that was up to her.

I spotted Agent Diaz's business card when I dumped the remains of Alex's letter into the trash. I'd tossed the card into the small basket I kept on the kitchen counter where I stored pens and notepaper and other bric-a-brac. I picked up the card and stared at it.

If I turned over the money to the FBI, could I do so without telling Agent Diaz about Alex's letter too? Agent Diaz would definitely question me. He'd want to know where I'd found the money and when and how. I couldn't lie. Lying to the FBI was a serious crime.

But Alex's letter had been sitting in my mailbox for days. I doubted he was still in San Diego. He was too smart to get caught so easily. He'd probably already crossed the border into Mexico. Or maybe he was living somewhere else under a false identity. Either way, telling Agent Diaz about the letter was not going to help the FBI find Alex.

At least that's what I told myself.

I WOKE up the next morning still thinking about Alex's letter and the money under my bathroom sink. I'd thought of little else since I'd found it. Although I'd returned to my aunt's house yesterday, I hadn't told my aunt about the money or the letter. And I didn't intend to. If there was ever any blowback, I wanted it to fall on me. This was my decision to make and my responsibility alone if I chose poorly.

As much as Alex wanted me to keep that money for MJ and Sofia, I knew I couldn't. It was drug money. The proceeds of a crime. I had to turn it over to the FBI. I had no choice. I just had to figure out how to do it without telling Agent Diaz about the letter too. Alex had all but confessed to the murder of Igor's crew in that letter. And even if he was no longer in San Diego, I didn't want to be the one to tell the FBI his last known whereabouts. The FBI would find Alex or they wouldn't, but I couldn't be the one to turn him in.

These were the thoughts running through my head as I sat in my doctor's office waiting room filling out forms with questions about my insurance coverage and my and my family's health history. When the nurse brought me into the exam room, she checked my weight, which was down, and my blood pressure, which was up. After the stress of the last few weeks neither surprised me. Then she instructed me to undress and change into the paper gown with the opening in the front.

I was staring up at the clouds painted on the exam room ceiling when Dr. Gartner walked in, clipboard in hand. "Grace, how are you? It's been a long time."

"It has," I acknowledged. She looked exactly the same as the last time I'd seen her, which had been for my post-partum checkup. Her dirty blond hair was still twisted into a messy bun on top of her head, she still wore oversized glasses although the frames had changed, and she still favored pale blue scrubs under her white doctor's coat.

"How's the baby?" she asked. "Although I guess she isn't a baby anymore."

I froze. I should've realized she would ask about Amelia. *Just rip off the bandage.* I swallowed hard and said, "She passed away."

Dr. Gartner's jaw dropped. "I'm so sorry, Grace, I had no idea."

I could feel the tears forming in my eyes, but I held them back. "I know. It's fine." *Please, please, please let's talk about something else. Anything else.*

She stammered for a few seconds, then asked, "Are you and your husband trying again? Not that you can ever replace a child but—"

I didn't want to have to tell her about Jonah too or answer

any questions about how they died. "No, I want to get back on the pill. Or I did when I made the appointment. I'm not sexually active right now so I don't really need them, but I'd like to get the prescription anyway. In case I need them down the road."

She didn't ask why a married woman was not sexually active. She probably assumed Jonah and I had divorced. The loss of a child had ended more than one marriage.

"Of course," she said. "Let me just examine you and make sure everything's okay." Then she set down her clipboard and pulled on her latex gloves.

We chatted about the weather while she gave me a breast exam, then I placed my feet in the stirrups and she asked me if I'd been to the marina lately. Several new restaurants had opened this summer, she told me, including a sushi place everyone was raving about. I told her I hadn't tried it yet.

"When was your last period?" she asked.

"A couple of weeks ago. I don't remember the exact date." Information she would know if she had bothered to read the forms I'd spent twenty minutes filling out in her waiting room.

"And everything was normal?"

"It was lighter than usual. But the last few months have been really stressful."

"Stress can definitely affect your cycle," she said as she reached for the ultrasound machine. "I just want to check something."

"Is everything okay?" I asked as she moved the wand around inside me.

She looked up and smiled. Then she removed the wand and pulled off her latex gloves. "Yes. You're pregnant."

Chapter 48

I STARED DUMBFOUNDED at Dr. Gartner.

"You're pregnant, Grace," she said again.

My mouth hung open until I eventually blurted out, "How did this happen?"

Dr. Gartner laughed. "I'm pretty sure you know how it happened."

"But we used protection."

"What did you use?" she asked.

"Condoms."

"Every time?"

I was about to say yes when I remembered that one night in the laundry room. Fuck! This could not be happening. And yet it was.

"I know this can be a bit overwhelming," Dr. Gartner said, "especially if you weren't expecting it. But you do have options. Do you want to go home and talk to the father and then we'll speak again?"

"The father's...not in the picture anymore."

"Are you sure? Because when something like this happens it can change things."

"I am one hundred percent positive. He's not even living in the country anymore." I didn't know if that was true, but I wasn't about to tell Dr. Gartner the father was either already on the FBI's Ten Most Wanted list or would be soon.

"Okay, then is there someone else you want to discuss it with? A friend or a family member? Not that you have to discuss it with anyone. The choice is entirely yours. But sometimes it's helpful to talk it over with someone when you're deciding what to do."

I nodded. "Yes. I'd like to do that."

"Good," she said and wheeled her stool to the other side of the room. She scribbled something on her clipboard then stood up. "You can get dressed. Just stop by the desk on your way out and tell them you need another appointment a month from now. If you decide you want to terminate the pregnancy, call and we'll schedule you sooner."

She had her hand on the doorknob when I stopped her. "Are you absolutely certain I'm pregnant? Maybe we should do a blood test to confirm. Because I really did have my period a couple of weeks ago. You can't be pregnant if you're still getting your period, right?"

"That wasn't your period, Grace. You were spotting. It's not uncommon in the first trimester. You're only six weeks along."

"Then you're sure I'm pregnant? Absolutely sure?"

"Do you want to hear the heartbeat?"

I told her I did not, then I dressed and left the office without stopping at the front desk. I'd call when I knew what I wanted to do.

The entire drive home I just had one thought running through my head over and over in an endless loop. *How could this have happened?* Of course, I knew the mechanics of it. Alex and I had sexual intercourse and in the heat of the moment we hadn't bothered to stop for a condom. But still. One time!

When I arrived back at my aunt's house, I found MJ and Sofia in the living room. MJ was playing a game on his Xbox and Sofia was sitting next to him on the floor building something with her Legos. I waved to them and ran up the steps, crashing into my mother in the hallway as she was leaving my aunt's bedroom.

"She's taking a nap," my mom said quietly as she shut my aunt's door. "PT was rough this morning. How was your appointment?"

"Fine," I said and continued down the hall to my own bedroom. I shut the door behind me and flopped facedown onto the bed.

Seconds later my mother knocked then stuck her head inside. "You don't look fine. You look a little pale."

"I'm fine, Mom. Really."

My mother walked in and sat down next to me on the bed. She placed her hand on my back and rubbed in circles like she used to when I was a little girl. That's when the tears came.

"I have bad news," I hiccupped between sobs.

"Oh my god, Grace, what did the doctor say? Tell me right this instant."

"I'm not sick," I said, realizing the conclusion she'd jumped to. "I'm perfectly healthy."

She placed her hand on her chest and blew out a breath, visibly relieved. "Oh, thank God. Then if you're not sick, what's wrong?"

"I'm pregnant."

Chapter 49

My mother laid down next to me on the bed and rubbed my back and told me, "It'll be alright," over and over again until I stopped crying. Then she held out the box of tissues and I plucked one and blew my nose.

"I can see you're not happy about this," she said, returning the tissue box to the nightstand, "but I'm not sure I understand why."

I sat up. "Are you kidding? Do you really not know who the father is?"

"Well, I assumed Alex."

"You assumed correct. So you see why this is a disaster."

"Um, no, actually, I don't."

I stared at her in amazement. "Your widowed daughter got herself knocked up by a murderer who's on the run from the FBI and you don't think that's a problem?"

"I'm not saying Alex would be my first choice for a son-in-law, but it's not as if you were ever going to marry him. I figured you were just going through a phase."

"A phase?"

"Yes. A lot of girls go through a bad boy phase. I did before I met your father. But you never did. I figured you were going through it now, and when you were done with Alex, you'd be back to your old self again."

I stared at my mother, truly at a loss for words. I never thought Alex and I had a future together. I knew that when I slept with him. And I was still coming to grips with my feelings about what he'd done. But Alex gave me something no one else could. He gave me justice for my family. He gave me peace of mind, or as close to it as I would ever get. To dismiss him as a phase? Alex meant much more to me than that.

"If you think about it," my mother continued, "Alex's leaving is really for the best. Now you can raise the baby yourself. You won't even have to tell anyone Alex is the father."

"And you're okay with the fact that I'd be having a child out of wedlock? That's not a sin anymore either?"

She waved her hand at me. "Honestly, Grace, it's the twenty-first century. No one's sending unwed mothers to homes anymore. Nowadays, women have babies on their own *on purpose*. My friend Cynthia's daughter just had a little boy a few months ago and she wasn't even dating anyone. Cynthia said she was tired of waiting around for Mr. Right so she went to a sperm bank and bought what she needed.

"Did you know they have books you look through that tell you all about the father? It's like ordering dinner. You can get exactly what you want. Anyway, I saw a picture of the baby and he's adorable. Alex was nice looking. I'm sure the two of you could make a very cute baby together."

"Who are you and what did you do with my mother?"

"I'm not as old-fashioned as you think. And in case you haven't noticed, neither one of us is getting any younger. Don't you think I'd like to be a grandmother again? Preferably while I'm still young enough to enjoy it."

And my mother was back.

We decided to tell my aunt about the pregnancy, but not the kids. Not yet anyway. Not until I decided what to do. My aunt's reaction was the same as my mother's, but it wasn't as shocking coming from her. She too wanted a new baby in the family.

I WOKE up early the next morning and left the house while everyone else was still asleep. I stopped at the grocery store to buy flowers, then drove to the cemetery. I sat down on the grass between the headstones like I always did, even though the ground was still wet with dew. "I know it's been a while," I said, "but it's been a really busy summer."

I told Jonah everything, including that I'd slept with Alex. I didn't know if telling your husband about your lover was proper etiquette, but it's not as if I was hurting his feelings. Then I told him about the pregnancy.

"It wasn't planned," I said. "Obviously. Even if I wanted to have a baby on my own, I never would've chosen Alex as the father. But he's not all bad. He has some good qualities too. He really does love MJ and Sofia and would do anything for them. That's a positive, isn't it?"

Jonah didn't answer, not that I expected him to.

"And if you can believe it," I continued, "my mother actually wants me to have a baby on my own. Apparently, she's gotten all progressive in her old age and now she's a cheerleader for single motherhood."

I laughed and shook my head. This was all so surreal.

"What do you think, Jonah? Should I have this baby?"

Chapter 50

One Year Later

I WALKED out of the family restroom with Emma in one arm, her favorite blanket in the other, and the overstuffed diaper bag slung over my shoulder. I knew the family restrooms were meant to be used by mothers with multiple children or fathers with babies because they didn't have changing tables in the men's restroom—Tim and Richard had told me that—but I liked to use them too because they had more space.

I hadn't spoken to Tim and Richard the entire time I'd been working for Igor because I didn't want to have to lie to them about why I was in LA. But I ran into Tim in the baby section of Target when I was five months pregnant, and we picked up where we'd left off as if no time had passed. He threw me a baby shower before Emma was born even though I told him not to, and just last week he signed us up for a Mommy and Me music class, although Tim insisted it should be called Parent and Me, and he was right about that. I knew Emma was too young for a music class, but I agreed to go because I wanted to start socializing with other parents again.

I decided to take my mother's advice and tell everyone I'd gone to a sperm bank and was a single mother by choice. It was easier that way. The only people who knew the truth were my mother and my aunt and I'd sworn them both to secrecy. I wondered sometimes if MJ suspected—Emma resembled me more than Alex except for her intense dark eyes, which she definitely inherited from him—but he never asked. I decided if he ever did, I would tell him the truth. I knew MJ could keep a secret.

The current debate at our house was whether we should continue to live there or buy a bigger one. Three bedrooms were sufficient when it was just me, MJ, and Sofia. But now that we had Emma too, I thought we needed a fourth bedroom, even though as MJ constantly reminded me, he was only going to be living with us for one more year and then he'd be off to college. We'd already planned tours to several schools in the fall.

Once Aunt Maddy was cleared to drive again and my foster parent application was approved, the kids and I moved out of my aunt's house and into mine. My local elementary school was better than the one in my aunt's neighborhood, although even in my school district it was a battle getting Sofia the resources she needed. The wealthier school districts didn't want to pay for services for kids with learning disabilities any more than the districts with less funding did. But I gave them no choice.

Aunt Maddy insisted she missed having us live with her, but I think she was secretly relieved. Although she'd recovered from her stroke, she didn't have as much energy as she used to. I also think she enjoyed having her freedom again. She and my mother were planning a wine tour through Europe for the end of the summer, and they were both bringing their respective boyfriends. My mother insisted at their age the appropriate term was "significant other." She'd met Bill Carson, a silver-haired widower, playing pickle ball and they'd hit it off right away.

Aunt Maddy was dating my former landlord Mike Murphy. I was shocked when she'd told me. I would never have imagined them as a couple. She said she hadn't imagined it either. Mike had spotted my aunt in the plumbing aisle of the local hardware store a few months ago. He recognized her from the times she'd visited me at my office, and he stopped to say hello and ask how I was doing. They went out for coffee and one thing led to another, and they've been together ever since. They were even talking about moving in together, but according to my aunt, no decision had been made yet.

I was the only one of the three of us who was still single. But I was the only one of the three of us with a fourteen-week-old baby. Apparently, unlike puppies, infants aren't a magnet for single men. I didn't care. I was smitten with Emma. I didn't need anyone else.

Since my arms were full, I pushed open the rec center door with my backside and smacked right into someone pulling the door open from the outside. I started to apologize when the man said, "Grace Keegan, right?"

"Yes." His face looked familiar, but in my sleep-deprived state, I couldn't place him.

"Nathan Hale," he said. "You beat me in court last year. Low-level drug offense. You got the judge to throw out my evidence then she dismissed the case."

I smiled as I remembered. It was a year and a half ago, the last time I'd been inside a courtroom. "I hope you're not holding a grudge."

"Definitely not," he said. "Although you did ruin my perfect record."

So he was holding a grudge. I understood. "Sorry about that."

"Dad, let's go," the boy standing next to him whined. He was wearing a blue basketball uniform and I guessed he was eight or nine years old.

"I don't want to keep you," I said and moved to the side, so I was no longer blocking the entrance.

Nathan glanced at his watch. "We have a few minutes."

The boy, who I assumed was his son, let out an exasperated sigh. Then he ran over to a group of boys wearing the same uniform, who were all watching a video on someone's phone.

Nathan sighed. "I'm still getting used to this schedule. It's my weekend."

"Your weekend?"

"Recently divorced," he said.

"Oh. I'm sorry to hear that. I'm a single parent too, but by choice."

"Wow, I couldn't imagine choosing this, especially at her age." He nodded at Emma. "It's a girl, right?"

I laughed. I always dressed Emma in pink when we left the house, so I didn't have to answer that question, but people asked anyway. "Yes, Emma." At the sound of her name, she started fussing. "I should probably go before she has a meltdown."

"Wait," he said. "Are you still working? Because I haven't seen you around the courthouse."

"I haven't been working recently but I'm planning on going back when Emma's a little older. Assuming I can find a job that's compatible with single motherhood." I was completely in love with Emma, but being a stay-at-home mother was not for me. The only thing I hated more than folding laundry was changing diapers.

"My offer still stands. If you ever want to join the other team, we're always looking for good lawyers. One of my colleagues just gave notice last week, so we'll be hiring soon."

Huh. I hadn't really given any thought to what kind of legal job I was going to look for, I just knew I needed to find one. I craved intellectual stimulation.

"The benefits are good," he continued, "and there's a daycare center in the building if that's of interest to you."

"Sold!"

Nathan laughed. "Great. Let me give you my card." He pulled a business card out of his wallet and tried to hand it to me, but my hands were full, so he stuffed it into the diaper bag instead.

"Dad, we need to go!" his son yelled as his teammates streamed into the rec center.

Nathan turned to me. "Call me and I can tell you more about the job. Or we could meet up for coffee if you want."

"Sure, that'd be great."

"I look forward to it," he said and jogged over to his son. The two of them followed the rest of the team inside.

I walked back to the blanket on the grass where I'd been sitting. Tim was still lounging there, but Richard and Sofia had taken Aaron, who was now a very energetic toddler, to the swings. Sofia couldn't wait for Emma to get older so she could play with her. Right now she treated Emma like a doll.

"Who was that?" Tim asked as soon as I sat down.

I cradled Emma in my arm and placed the bottle into her mouth. When she was contentedly sucking, I turned to Tim. "You mean the guy I was talking to? He's a lawyer. We met last year. He said his office is hiring and he thinks I should apply."

"Are you going to?" he asked.

Unlike me, Tim was happy being a stay-at-home parent. He was pushing Richard to adopt another baby. "Maybe. He gave me his card and told me to call him so we could meet up for coffee to discuss it."

Tim raised one eyebrow. "Oh, really."

I scoffed. "Yes, Tim, we're actually going to talk about the job. Some of us like working."

"Sounds like an excuse to me. Did you happen to notice if he was wearing a wedding ring?"

"I didn't, but he told me he was recently divorced."

Now both of his eyebrows shot up. "He just slipped that into the conversation, did he?"

I laughed. "Yes, as a matter of fact he did. And I told him I was a single parent by choice."

"Good girl. When are you going to call him?"

"I don't know. Next week, maybe?"

"Don't wait too long. The good ones don't stay single for long."

I intended to call Nathan, but about the job. I wasn't looking for romance. I was content with my life. That realization shocked me. *I was content with my life.* When Jonah and Amelia died, I thought my life was over. But it wasn't over. It just changed. My life had not unfolded the way I'd imagined it would, but it was still a good life.

I stared down at Emma, who had drifted off to sleep in my arms. My life was filled with love again, and that was all I needed.

A Note from the Author

Thank you so much for reading the *Fall from Grace* series. I sincerely hope you enjoyed the books. If you've read any of my earlier works (mostly rom-coms and humorous mysteries), you know this series was a bit of a departure for me. But sometimes a character lodges in an author's head and refuses to leave until their story is told, and that's what happened here.

For those of you who aren't quite ready to let go of these characters, I've written a bonus epilogue for my newsletter subscribers. It takes place five years after the end of this book (i.e., six years after Alex disappears). I'll give you a hint—Alex is still alive. If you'd like to read the bonus epilogue, you can sign up to receive a digital copy at the web address below.

Exclusive Bonus Epilogue: subscribepage.io/BDKj8e

I love hearing from readers! Feel free to visit me at www.bethorsoff.com and tell me what you thought of the books. Or if you wouldn't mind leaving a review online that would be great too. Reviews are crucial for indie authors because we don't have publicity departments pushing our books out to the world. If you liked the books, please spread the word!

Thank you.

About the Author

Beth Orsoff is an Amazon bestseller and the author of twelve novels ranging from romantic comedies to domestic suspense. She lives in Los Angeles with her child, a fish, and a cat who is trying to eat the fish. You can reach Beth online at www.bethorsoff.com.

www.ingramcontent.com/pod-product-compliance
Lightning Source LLC
Chambersburg PA
CBHW020022310726
48970CB00007B/2166

* 9 7 9 8 9 8 8 7 3 2 9 2 1 *